The night ha~~d~~
a terrible mist~~ake~~!

True, it had seemed magical at the time, but that was just the influence of the moonlight and the wine, wasn't it?

Susanna drew a deep breath. "Mr. Arne, we have nothing to say to each other. I'm ashamed to admit I was, well, a little under the weather when we met in the woods last night. Otherwise, I wouldn't have dreamed of going to your house—"

"But I have a great deal to say to you, Susanna," he interrupted smoothly.

Summoning all her dignity, she intoned coolly, "I deeply regret what happened last night—"

"Do you now?" Once again he cut in, preventing her from finishing. "And what *did* happen last night?" he went on. "You don't know, do you?"

Susanna felt herself grow warm with embarrassment....

Diana Hamilton creates high-tension conflict that brings new life to traditional romance. Readers will no doubt find her a welcome addition to the Harlequin program and will be glad to know that more novels by this talented author are already in the works.

Books by Diana Hamilton

HARLEQUIN PRESENTS
993—SONG IN A STRANGE LAND

Don't miss any of our special offers. Write to us at the following address for information on our newest releases.

Harlequin Reader Service
901 Fuhrmann Blvd., P.O. Box 1397, Buffalo, NY 14240
Canadian address: P.O. Box 603,
Fort Erie, Ont. L2A 5X3

Impulsive Attraction

Diana Hamilton

Harlequin Books

TORONTO • NEW YORK • LONDON
AMSTERDAM • PARIS • SYDNEY • HAMBURG
STOCKHOLM • ATHENS • TOKYO • MILAN

Original hardcover edition published in 1987
by Mills & Boon Limited

ISBN 0-373-02865-2

Harlequin Romance first edition October 1987

CHAPTER ONE

Susanna Bryce-Jones was bored, her mood approaching edginess. Both states of mind were alien to her. They puzzled her. She was not a giddy twenty-year-old, given to restlessness; she was a mature, sensible woman, always in control.

A tall girl, she could see clear over the heads of the group of twittering, clacking, yapping females, whose resemblance to a horde of French poodles irritated her so, to where Edmond stood, glass in hand, his mid-brown neat head deferentially tilted as he listened to the bass rumble of conversation from his impeccably lounge-suited male companions.

Edmond, at least, appeared to be enjoying himself, she thought sourly, helping herself to another glass of white wine from the Chippendale sideboard. Her third or her fourth? Susanna had lost count. This party was driving her to drink, and as she didn't normally drink much, a vague feeling of unease crept through her, almost immediately overlaid by a belligerent couldn't-care-less-ness.

Normally she cared very much about her behaviour, about the way she was viewed by other people. And consideration for others constituted good manners, and good manners indicated good breeding. It was a tenet her mother had instilled in her, practically from birth, and Susanna, who was

5

an only and properly brought up offspring of parents whose standing in the county was high, usually adhered to it. But right now she felt out of sorts, and quite uncharacteristically rebellious.

Edmond had been enormously gratified—his words—when they'd been invited to this party. Everyone who was anyone in the small country town of Much Barton would be there. They had obviously 'arrived', Edmond had preened; she, the first female bank manager the small community had experienced, and he, an ambitious, youngish chartered accountant who had recently set up shop in rooms above the library, had both obviously been accepted into the upper hierarchy of the town.

Susanna hadn't actively *not* wanted to come, but she hadn't been enthusiastic. And that wasn't too surprising, because she saved her enthusiasm for her work. She hadn't been properly excited about her recent engagement to Edmond. Her mother had been excited enough for the two of them. But now Susanna had been here for two hours, listening to the babble of chatter from the self-segregated groups, male and female, the county accents growing more shrill as the drink circulated, and she wanted out.

The room was unbearably hot. And the French windows were open to the warm late-June night. Her hazel eyes narrowing, Susanna wondered whether she could make a bid for freedom without being seen. The trouble with being an Amazon, she thought wryly, was that one was so difficult to overlook!

But she made it, edging round the wife of a retired Colonel, who was resplendent in multi-coloured chiffon, easing herself carefully down the single step to the terrace, breathing a tremendous sigh of relief as the fresher air whispered against her heated skin.

Still clutching her glass of wine, she idled over the paving stones to where a shallow flight of stairs, marked by geranium-filled urns, led down to an expanse of smoothly cut lawn. She wouldn't stay long, she promised herself; just long enough to cool down and get over her unnecessary ill humour. To have deliberately held herself aloof from her hosts, the Anstruthers, and the other guests whose smug, self-congratulatory conversation and attitudes had so unaccountably aggravated her, was bad enough. To deliberately sneak away was another matter entirely. Unpardonable rudeness, Edmond would say, and he would be right. And what her mother would have to say, should she ever get to hear about it—which, of course, she wouldn't—didn't bear thinking about.

She negotiated the steps, wincing. Her new shoes—flat heels because at five-foot-eleven she already topped Edmond by an inch—hurt horribly.

After taking a sip of her wine, she eased off the offending items and smiled blissfully as her nylon-clad toes curled in the cool short grass. That was much better. Another sip of wine and she felt better still, and half-way down the lawn she very carefully placed her glass on an obliging sundial, removed her cut-off jacket and dropped it to the ground. Better still. Her mother called it a bolero but Susanna, who always called a spade a spade, called it a cut-off jacket. 'Keep it on,' her mother had advised. 'Then there won't be so much of you on show.'

Peering down in the amethyst-tinted moonlight, Susanna had to concede that her parent had a point. With the concealing jacket removed, the draped bodice of the silky black dress—secured by only the narrowest of straps—did reveal an amazing amount of flesh. But then, she thought drearily, she *carried* an amazing amount of flesh.

That particular thought demanded the consolation of another sip of wine. One sip led to another, and she replaced the empty glass on the sundial with regret and wavered her way further down the lawn.

It wasn't that she minded about being a big girl, not in the least. She didn't have any hang-ups, she reminded herself firmly. She had come to terms with her size at the age of thirteen when her mother, who had never ceased to be surprised at having produced a daughter so unlike her petite and slenderly elegant self, had taken her to one side. 'Unfortunately, dear, you must never hope to rely on your looks to smooth your way through life. But you do have brains. Use them.'

And Susanna had. She had made herself stop minding the pitying looks of the girls at school, the dismissive looks of the boys, had cultivated a lack of interest in fashion and fun until the graft had become a staunch, well-rooted plant, and had applied her brain to the worthwhile task of making her way in life.

Brilliant in her way, she had walked away from the LSE with a degree in economics, joined the management stream of the Shire Counties Bank, sailed through her two years of intensive training and her Institute of Bankers exams. And at the unprecedented early age of twenty-eight she had been promoted to the position of manager at the Much Barton branch.

Which wasn't bad going, not by anyone's standards it wasn't.

So why the sour mood, the feeling of restlessness that was hitherto unknown to her? She had everything going for her. A good job with dizzying prospects if she wished to push her career to the limits. A newly acquired home of her own. A prospective husband who was sensible, secure, presentable and, if what her mother said was anything to go by, a Golden Opportunity. For who in the world would have expected any man to fall in love with the brainy, big, plain Susanna Bryce-Jones?

But did Edmond love her? she wondered dully as she came to a wicket gate in the fence which bordered the Anstruthers' garden. Or had his offer of marriage been prompted by the fact that her father, a self-made businessman turned country landowner and her mother, 'upper-middle county', were both financially very well-heeled, possessed of only one child and not likely, at this stage of their lives, to have another?

She didn't suppose she would ever know. On that depressing thought she lifted the latch on the gate and pushed it open. Behind her lay the lighted house, the boring party, and Edmond. In front of her lay woodland, dark and mysterious, but not dense enough to deflect the shafts of cool pure moonlight that fingered the canopy of leaves, slanting through to the small silvery green glades that now beckoned so enticingly.

There was no competition, she admitted, pushing through ferns that whispered in her wake. Better to stay out here for a while, unwind, then go back to the dreadful party and wait until Edmond was ready to drive her home.

Besides, he wouldn't miss her. She wasn't the type men worried about, anguished over. Missed.

And, strangely enough, she wasn't missing him. In
fact, she decided as an owl hooted eerily, making
her smile, she was actually glad he wasn't here
with her. Edmond didn't like the great outdoors. It
was undisciplined and untidy, laid traps for the
unwary. While Susanna, to her mild astonishment,
found herself thoroughly enjoying the dapple of
moonlight on bark and leaves, the feel of the
rough earth beneath her feet, the scent of trees
and water.

And there *was* water! She tottered down a
shallow bank to a smooth-running stream, oily dark
but sparked to diamond brilliance here and there
where moonlight spilled.

Susanna wasn't an impulsive girl, but she was
breaking records tonight, she decided as she
dropped down on the mossy bank and wriggled out
of her tights. Testing the water with one bare foot,
she discovered it was blessedly cool, silky and
strangely sensuous. Bliss! With two feet in now,
she waded downstream until the water swirled
around her knees, and she chuckled, holding her
skirts up around her thighs, clear of the stream.

She felt more like a child than she'd done when
she'd actually been a child, she acknowledged to
herself with a slightly tipsy giggle. She had always
been so much bigger and heavier than her peers,
had never seemed able to fit in with them, and the
older children hadn't wanted her tagging along, so
her childhood had been lonely and she had spent
most of her time with her head stuck in a book or
playing chess with her grandfather when he'd been
alive. And now, at twenty-eight years of age, she
was rapidly discovering that feeling like a child
again, just for once, was fun.

There must be enchantment abroad in the night

air, drifting down on the moonbeams, to have changed the sober, industrious, totally sensible bank manager into a carefree child, she thought, grinning at the fanciful and unprecedented turn her mind was taking.

She was in a deeper part of the stream now, almost a pool, the tree-hung banks further apart, the moon reflecting a shiny white light on the still surface of the water. With a feeling that was almost pagan in its abandonment, Susanna dropped her skirts, careless of the inevitable wetting, and shivered deliciously as the water pressed the wet fabric against her thighs.

Lifting her arms, her full breasts straining against the thin fabric of her dress, she tugged the pins from her hair, releasing it from the demure knot at her nape, shaking her head slowly so that the heavy seal-brown mane swung this way and that, a dusky, silky cloud, the moonlight filtering through.

'Magnificent! Superb!' The deep male voice was slow, husky, intimately caressing, and Susanna, almost—but not quite—shocked back to cold sobriety, slowly dropped her arms and crossed them over her breasts, peering owlishly through her drifting hair for the source of the voice. A shadowy form moved from the darkness beneath the trees into full moonlight, and Susanna's breath caught in her throat.

If he was a flesh and blood man, and not a product of her wine-hazed imagination, then he had to be the most perfect specimen she'd ever seen. The silvery light painted his strong male physique in bold brush strokes of black and white; his clothes could have been skin-tight or a suit of shimmering armour, his hair, above his shadowed eyes, a helmet of silver gilt.

Her breath fluttered uncertainly, and the sensation that she might just have stumbled, somehow, into a magical place flittered around inside her head like a half-crazed bat.

'Who are you?' Even her voice didn't sound like her own. The precise, cool tones were displaced by a tendency to throaty invitation that implied far more than the simple enquiry.

He moved his head once in slow negation and came forward again, further down the bank above her, the sureness of his movements, the play of hard muscle and bone modelled boldly and fluidly in the wash of moonlight and shadow.

'I watched you walk through the water and wondered if the old gods were wakeful tonight. Aphrodite by moonlight—or Juno, dropped from the heavens to walk with mortals?' He planted his bare feet wide, just touching the lapping rim of water. 'What *is* your name?'

'Susanna.' No power on earth could have forced her to withhold it. His shadowed eyes held her in thrall, drawing her on to his plane, to a place she had never visited before this night. And her heart thudded heavily, following the drum-beat rhythm of another dimension in time and space as he commanded softly,

'Come here, Susanna.'

She went, mindlessly pushing across the pool, water creeping up to her hips, moulding her body with its ambient strength. His hands were held out to her and she took them, her fingers curling around their muscular structure, grasping the living warmth of skin and flesh and bone, feeling his grip tighten and pull her forwards as she moved steadily up the fern-grown bank, water streaming from her skirts, plastering the fabric to her hips and thighs.

Standing in front of him, their mutual handclasp keeping them bonded, she breathed deeply, steadily, accepting the quality of magic that haunted the night, the man, her own self. He was taller than she by a good four or five inches. A god-like figure, powerfully built yet possessing a lithe, almost feline quality that set him apart. His face was still in shadows, untouched by the moonglow, but his hair, dropping haphazardly on to his forehead, was touched with brilliant silver light.

'You are beautiful.'

His voice, deep and slow and warm, caressed her like the intimate touch of a lover and exactly echoed the thought that had formulated in her mind in regard to him. And the sentiment he expressed didn't seem ridiculous or false, because it was part of the magic of a night when the world seemed to have tilted on its axis, throwing up new perspectives, opening on to the realms of fantasy. A night when pumpkins could turn into coaches, when circumspection receded to the Land of Boredom where it belonged, when large plain girls became beautiful princesses, and gods and goddesses walked abroad . . .

'Now tell me, Susanna, what were you doing in my fridge?'

The absurdity of his words, her own chimes of delighted laughter, splintered the spell, and Susanna didn't know whether to be glad or sorry. Glad, she supposed, on the whole. At least it proved she wasn't mad, or drunk—not totally, anyway. And he was a flesh and blood man, not a reincarnation of an ancient wild wood-god, and she wasn't an enchanted princess—she was plain Susanna Bryce-Jones, who had wandered away from a party, paddled in a stream and found a man who talked in riddles.

'I don't have a fridge at home.' He released her hands and moved away, leaving her feeling inexplicably cold. 'So when I want my wine chilled I leave it here.'

He was on his haunches now, strong hands moving deftly amongst the ferns at the water's edge, and he straightened up and she could hear the smiling challenge in his voice. 'Share the wine with me, Susanna?'

Something new and unexpected unfurled inside her, the sharply sweet sensation of excitement, the gauntlet of the unknown, the need to hold on to the last lingering hope that magic existed somewhere. Tomorrow she would be her sanely prosaic self again, but tonight was for dreaming, surely it was, set aside for the madness of enchantment.

'Thank you.' She pushed a silken swathe of heavy hair back from her face with a hand that shook a little. 'You haven't told me your name.'

'Is that important?' He had moved closer, holding the bottle in one hand, the other tucking the drifting hem of his grey shirt into the waistline of his body-hugging denim jeans.

'Nice girls don't share bottles of wine with strangers.' She was smiling, she couldn't seem to stop smiling, and he must have seen because his white teeth showed in a sudden answering grin.

'You must have missed a lot in life, Susanna! It's Jackson. Jackson Arne. Come on.' He held out a hand and she took it without hesitation.

'Where to?'

'Home to my place.'

'Why?' She could feel his eyes on her, sliding from her upturned face to the gleaming shoulders, the upper curves of the full breasts the black dress left bare, and for the first time since she'd left the party she felt self-conscious, aware of the way the wet dress clung, leaving little to the imagination. She felt oddly vulnerable, wide open to a whole new world of uncharted emotion, too aware, suddenly, of the body she'd learned to ignore—except for its need to be fed and washed and clothed. Someone, in her first year of training, had called her 'billowy', but Jackson said thickly, 'God—you are magnificent!'

Slowly, he reached out a hand, strong fingers tracing the contours of her collar bones, feathering downwards over the ripe swelling of her upper breasts, his fingers supple, enquiring, moving over her flesh as a blind man might learn to know a work of three-dimensional art. And everywhere his fingers touched they left behind a sensation exquisite enough to scorch and sear, flooding her body with spiralling warmth. And when he walked away, taking a well-trodden path between the trees, her feeling of loss was deep enough to make her want to cry.

'It isn't far,' he threw at her over his shoulder, and Susanna stamped her foot, suffused with a cross-grained emotion she couldn't put a name to, forgetting she wasn't wearing shoes, screwing her face up as her tender instep made contact with something hard and sharp.

'Why go to your place? Why not stay here?' Her voice was husky with pain and loss and possibly rage. Because it was one thing to drink wine with an intriguing stranger on the banks of a stream, within shouting distance of a house and people, quite another to wander off into the darkness of night with him.

He turned, and it was difficult to tell in the dappled moonlight whether his face was contorted with laughter or frustrated evil.

'Because, gorgeous Susanna, the corkscrew is there, not to mention glasses. And your dress is very wet. Don't you want to dry it before going home? Where do you live, anyway?'

He asked this as if it were an afterthought, slipping out against his will, as though he didn't really care to know. The words 'Ships that pass in the night' trickled through her brain and she recalled that he hadn't seemed too eager to introduce himself, a suspicion that was reinforced when he walked on again, adding lightly, 'Forget I asked. It's none of my business where you live.'

'Mallow Cottage—it's just out of Much Barton, on the Ludcote road,' she told him anyway, her feet drawing her along the path he was taking as if they had a mind of their own. 'I only moved in there three weeks ago. I'd lived in London before. But then I was promoted, given the management of the Much Barton branch—I work for Shire Counties Banks—and I had to move in with my parents—they live near Ludcote, twenty miles away—and of course I needed to be nearer my work, and I wanted to be independent—who doesn't!' She was babbling, a thing she never did, and she was telling a stranger her life story, and she never did that, either.

He didn't comment, he just walked ahead, easily, noiselessly, and she had the strangest feeling that he could vanish at any moment, dissolve into the darkness beneath the trees, that he was, after all, a figment of her imagination, a creature called up out of a subconscious desire for a little magic in her life. She didn't want him to be that. And perhaps he was right in not commenting about the personal data she'd spilled out, not asking more questions. They were strangers who had met under strange circumstances on a warm, moonlit night. To dwell on the minutiae of placement, status, background, would be to shatter the illusion of enchantment and bring a magical encounter down to the plane of the mundane.

It wasn't as if they would ever meet again; they would have no occasion to, surely, and this was a night out of time, an adventure which wouldn't be repeated.

Panting, out of breath with her efforts to keep up with him because although he moved effortlessly they had covered quite a stretch of ground, she cannoned into him as he stopped at the edge of the wooded area.

His arms steadied her, the action pulling her body close to his, and warmth flooded her clear down the side that was held to his body; she wondered if that had anything to do with the way her heart picked up speed, racing, conveying fast rivulets of hot sensation through her limbs, right down to her bare toes which curled convulsively in the cool grass.

'There—it wasn't far, was it?'

They had emerged on the edge of a small meadow. Pale mist was rising from the grass, hazing the outlines of a squat, higgledy-piggledy building, and Susanna wrenched her mind away from the bemused contemplation of the strange things that were happening to her body for long enough to ask, 'Is that your place?'

'I don't own it, if that's what you mean. I'm just shacking up there for a time. Let's go inside and see if we can get you dry again.' The hand that had been splayed around her waist dropped to her hip, patting gently to underline his statement, and the warmth of him seared through the wet clinging fabric of her dress, making her gasp.

He began to walk, his hand returning to her waist, supporting her. And she needed support. She felt weak, boneless, and leant against him, matching her steps to his with difficulty, her right breast pressed against his warm ribcage, her left heavy, aching for his strong fingers to move upwards in a caress.

She had never experienced such feelings before, she acknowledged bemusedly, shocked by her own body's wanton reactions to him. It was as if she were no longer in charge of herself. But tonight had been set apart for strange new happenings. She had instinctively known that from the moment she'd entered the wood. And the conviction had been reinforced, made true, when he'd spoken to her, called her beautiful.

Tomorrow, and all the other tomorrows of her life, would be as sane and sensible and proper as all her yesterdays had been . . . and dull?

And he wasn't trying to take advantage of her, and he had no way of knowing how he was affecting her because she was the only one who knew that, and she wasn't telling him! If he chose to make love to her she'd probably end up encouraging him—in the odd moon-kissed mood she was in tonight.

Apart from the way he'd touched her shoulders and chest—in retrospect, the quality of the movement of his fingers over her skin had been academic—he hadn't done a thing she could possibly take exception to. And she didn't know whether to be disappointed by that or not. Not, she supposed.

She was a nice, well-brought-up young woman, wasn't she? And she was engaged to marry Edmond and shouldn't be thinking this way about any other man, and just because Jackson had said flattering things to her and no one else ever had—except in regard to her brain power—and just because his merest touch flooded her with dizzying sensation and Edmond, the only man who'd ever kissed her, make her feel awkward and clumsy and a tiny bit silly—didn't mean she had to throw herself at his head.

'Mind how you go; there's a step right here.'

Her feet fumbled over the threshold of an open door, set into stone walls. He went ahead, and she heard his sure-footed movements in the darkness, the scrape and flare of a match, and then the golden light grew, enlarging until it filled most of the room, and she saw his face clearly for the first time as he replaced the pearly glass globe over the wick of the oil lamp.

He wasn't a conventional man—in her short time of knowing him she'd recognised that—and he wasn't conventionally handsome. No pure chiselled features of a fairy-tale prince. But his face had humour, warmth, strength. Broad Slavic cheekbones were thrown into prominence by the lamplight; a straight nose, though slightly off-centre as if he'd broken it at one time. In a fight? The jawline suggested aggression, and the quirky, wide mouth with its thin upper lip and slightly too-full lower spoke of hard determination coupled with wilfulness.

He didn't apologise for the abysmally cluttered state of the room. Susanna would have felt *abject* if anyone had walked in and found her home in such confusion. And she should have been feeling embarrassed for his sake, but she wasn't.

Jackson knelt and put a match to the kindling and logs in the deep stone hearth, and she knew that tonight she was capable of accepting anything, without question. That was so unlike the self she knew that she felt a laugh rising inside her like champagne bubbles.

'I'll find something for you to wear while your dress dries.'

His rich warm voice brought her eyes winging open, the lamplight drawing golden flecks from the deep hazel depths as she looked up at him, her heavy hair swirling silkily back from her face. He seemed to tower above her, the breadth of his shoulders underlining his aura of power, strength and determination. And for the first time in her entire life Susanna felt small and fragile. It was a heady experience, and the bubble of laughter inside her burst, escaping her lips in a throaty chuckle.

Jackson brushed her jawline gently, with a giant fist, and he laughed softly, as if he understood, then shrugged, turning. There was a narrow flight of stairs set beside the chimney alcove; he disappeared, and she could hear him moving around over the floorboards that straddled the beams of the low ceiling above her head.

Susanna moved to the hearth, past the shabby squashy sofa, covered with piles of books, and spread out her skirts to the beginnings of heat from the flames which licked at apple logs, releasing the trapped scents of decades of summers past.

He was down again in seconds, his large hands holding something golden and silky. He tossed it carelessly on top of one of the piles of books on the sofa, his smile crooked.

'Put that on while I find clean glasses. Won't be a tick.'

He wove his way through the cluttered furniture, his bare feet soundless on the boards, disappearing through a low wood-planked door, ducking his head, and Susanna wrenched at the zip at the back of her dress, stepping out of it and covering her sensible cotton underwear with his robe.

She knew it was his. The fabric held his smell—male and slightly spicy—and she rolled the too-long sleeves up and tied the belt around her waist, conscious of how the silky fabric clung.

His name was Jackson Arne. She wrinkled her brow, staring into the flames, wondering where she'd heard it before. It seemed familiar, somehow. Shrugging, she dismissed the vague puzzle and spread her wet and ruined dress over a chunky ugly table near the fire to dry. His name probably seemed familiar because, like the rest of this night's happenings, it was strange but somehow right. Known and yet unknown. And it was all too much for her mind which, she acknowledged wryly, was already just a little fuddled with alcohol.

He came back with the wine and two glasses, his eyes sweeping her, approving. Making room on a table top, pushing aside a tottering pile of magazines, he turned his back on her, pouring the wine, and Susanna's eyes devoured him.

My, but he's broad, she appraised, her lashes flickering as her eyes travelled down from the wide muscular shoulders, straight back, trim waist. The shabby, frayed jeans he wore were belted low on narrow hips, clinging where they covered long, long legs . . .

'There you go.' He turned round, holding out a glass, and her eyes snapped wide again then crinkled into a grin that echoed his as she took the

wine. 'I'm afraid you'll have to make do with a
tumbler, I've nothing more elegant.'

The thick tall glass was brimming, and Susanna
drank some of the pale golden liquid, the wine
sharp, tasting of grapes and sunshine, sliding down
her throat like cold silk. He bent, moving the piles
of books from the sofa and dumping them on the
floor, and the lamplight glanced over his head,
gilding the unruly honey-gold hair. She wanted to
touch, to tangle her fingers in its thickness, in the
crispness where the hair curled into the tanned
nape of his neck. But she knew that would be
asking for trouble, trouble that not even the new
and reckless self that had been conjured out of this
night could deal with. Besides, she was engaged to
marry Edmond, so she had no right to be thinking
of this man in *that* way. No right at all. And after
tonight she wouldn't.

'Make yourself comfortable,' he told her, smiling
his lazy smile, the deep green eyes softly narrowed,
his golden head slightly tilted as she dropped on to
the sofa and tucked her long legs beneath her. She
wondered with half-fearful anticipation whether he
would join her, and although she was very well
aware that it would be better if he didn't, she was
disproportionately dejected when he didn't, when
he took his glass and assumed an arrogant straddle-
legged stance in front of the fire. But her brief low
mood didn't last long, not when she saw how he
didn't take his eyes off her, the look they held
making her feel warm inside.

'So what were you doing, wading down that
stream!' His eyes caught the glint when the hoop
of diamonds on her wedding finger winked slyly as
she lifted her glass to sip the wine. 'Alone,' he
added heavily.

'Oh, Edmond,' she dismissed, catching his drift. 'I left him at a boring party, I'm afraid. In any case, he wouldn't have joined me in the stream, he wouldn't have done anything so . . . silly?' Her voice questioned and she searched his eyes to see if he endorsed her choice of word. But she could read nothing from his narrowed eyes because the glow of lamplight, though mellow and pleasing, didn't reach them.

'Tell me about yourself?' He put his glass down on the hearth, and a corner of her mind registered the fact that he'd barely touched the contents. She sighed, contented, sipping more wine, then settled back comfortably. Drowsy and content, she analysed her feelings—the slow warmth spreading through her, coupled with the delicious and definitely discernible undertones of prickly excitement was attributable, she knew, to the compelling immediacy of his effect on her—more than to the wine she had consumed or the feeling of recklessness engendered by her ill-mannered truancy.

'What do you want to know?'

'Anything. Everything. As little or as much as you want to tell me. Just talk.'

So she did. The words came easily, tripping off her tongue as she told him of the elegant Queen Anne house her father had bought with excess profits, the acres and acres of land, the tenant farmers he enjoyed 'overseeing'. Her father would have liked a son to inherit, or a daughter who at the very least reproduced her mother's looks and sophistication. Failing that, he hadn't wanted to know, except, just lately, when he saw the hope of a grandson when she'd agreed to marry Edmond. So, in getting engaged to Edmond she had earned her father's reserved approval at last. Not that it really mattered to her, of course; she was her own woman. She had a good job with better prospects and a home of her own. And agreeing to marry Edmond hadn't been a way of gaining her parents' approval. No way. Oh, no. Edmond was a good sort, steady and kind, and she wanted a family because she wasn't *absolutely* sure that a career would be enough. There hadn't been much affection in her life, not since her grandfather had died. Not that she'd suffered from the lack of it, but children, hordes of them, would bring her that. Though she wasn't sure if Edmond wanted *hordes*. He had mentioned two. Some time.

Jackson hadn't commented as she'd rambled on, and she wondered if he'd stopped listening when he'd discovered that what she had to say on the dreary subject of herself was so frightfully boring. He'd refilled her glass, though, and now it was empty again, so she must have consumed the lion's share of the bottle . . . And on top of the wine she'd had at the Anstruthers' . . . Was he by any chance trying to get her drunk? Well, he had succeeded, she thought muzzily as the room began to waltz around . . .

'Stand up, Susanna, would you?'

Perhaps the request wasn't *too* odd, she mused ponderously, wrinkling her brow, having great difficulty now putting her thoughts into any kind of coherent order. Maybe he was hinting that it was time she went home? Or maybe he just wanted to know if she *could* stand?

She could. Just. And her eyes blinked owlishly up at him. He was looking at her in a very peculiar way, as if he were holding a conversation with himself inside his head, his eyes inward-looking, the hard muscles of his chest and shoulders bunched with concentration.

'Now put your weight on your right hip, Susanna—and relax your left knee just a little. Yes, that's fine.' He prowled around her, his green eyes raking her from head to toe, his wide lower lip sucked in, caught between his teeth. 'Could you lift your arms? Both of them. That's right—now clasp your hands behind your head, lifting your hair.'

She did as he asked simply because, she admitted hazily, she didn't have the wits not to. The way he was stalking around her, looking, unnerved her completely—when she stopped to really think about it. And she was beginning to feel rather ill.

With a sudden and horrifying insight she saw what a sight she must look. Her large face framed with mussed up hair, two large bosoms thrusting upwards, one large hip stuck out! And what did he think he was doing, dammit? Was he mad? Quite probably! She was, in any case; she had to be crazy to come following him here, her big senseless feet bumbling along, carrying her into goodness only knew what kind of funny set-up!

He'd told her he was shacking up here. Did he by any chance mean squatting? Very probably. And the mess he lived in! The tatty old jeans and shirt he was wearing! No proper wine glasses! The funny way he was eyeing her—almost as if he were wondering how many joints she'd cut up into! The way her head was spinning, the room out of control . . . Susanna began to feel very ill indeed.

She dropped her arms and he said 'Right!' his voice husky with barely controlled excitement. 'Exactly right. Perfect. I want you, Susanna!'

She gaped, knowing she must look like an idiot,

an inebriated idiot at that, but unable to do a thing about it. 'I want you' needed no explanation, and the picture those words had implanted in her mind made her stomach lurch over with a white, sharp feeling that wasn't entirely unpleasant. But right for *what*? A perfect *what*? her mind shrieked.

A perfect imbecile to put herself into this dreadful situation, that's what, her mind wailed back at her.

Pushing past him, her feet plaiting, she made a grab for her still-damp dress, dropped it, looked around for her shoes, then remembered she'd left them in the middle of the Anstruthers' immaculate lawn.

Oh my lordy! She'd never find her way back to retrieve them and walk the one mile home, not in the state she was in. Always presuming, of course, that this—this suddenly quite unnerving man allowed her out of his door!

She made a determined effort to pull herself together.

'I have to go home now, Mr Arne. Thank you for the wine, but I really do have to go.'

The words came out with enormous dignity, she felt, hearing them roll with careful enunciation from her tongue, but she was ashamed when she let herself down by stumbling over the pile of books and landing in an untidy heap back on the sofa.

'You don't seem to be in any fit state to go anywhere.'

He was laughing at her, damn him! She could hear it in his rich warm voice, see—if she squinted with her head at *precisely* the right angle—the way his mouth curled up at one side more than the other when he grinned.

Fat tears gathered hotly in her eyes, and try as she might she could do nothing about the humiliating way her chin quivered so childishly, and she didn't know whether it was worse to be laughed at or seduced, which was probably what he'd had in mind when he'd lured her here and plied her with drink!

Susanna knuckled her eyes and cursed her luck at having picked the one man she'd ever met who was bigger than she to go moon-crazy with. She could bulldoze her way through most men she knew. But not this one.

'Come on, Susanna.' Two strong hands reached out for her, lifting her up to her feet quite effortlessly, his arms sliding round to hold her, gentling her. And she thought dizzily, as her head fell against the area of his chest which his buttonless shirt left bare and she felt the tickle of golden hair beneath her wet cheek, that she was going to need all her wits about her if she were to get out of this shocking and very humiliating situation in one piece.

The only trouble was, her wits had all abandoned her, and he had said he wanted her, and he had the look of a man who always got exactly what he wanted!

CHAPTER TWO

'YES, Penny,' said Susanna with careful levelness, 'I'll see Mr Harding. Show him through in a couple of minutes, would you?' Her smile was stiff as the clerk withdrew from the office. It hurt to smile. She had woken with a terrible headache and an enormous burden of shame. How could she have behaved so stupidly last night? How could she? She, of all people!

She had to put it right behind her. Try to forget it had ever happened. And face Edmond and try to apologise.

All through this long, difficult day she had been expecting Edmond to call in or phone her. And it *had* been difficult to get through her normal workload while her head pounded and her stomach heaved. And that elderly couple, the Grants, who'd asked to see her for advice on investment accounts, had kept talking and talking, obviously more interested in seeing how a female bank manager shaped up than in learning how to get more out of their life savings.

She didn't measure up to much today, she felt, as she patted her hair to reassure herself that it was still as it should be, neatly coiled at the back of her head, no stray strands escaping. Just a stupid female who had followed a figment of her imagination, only to find the reality of a somehow dangerous man in frayed jeans who was squatting in a near-derelict hovel, who'd plied her with drink, who'd . . .

Her mind blanked off smartly as Edmond entered her office. He must never find out the truth about last night. For him to know would be too shaming. Her own self-image was as low as it could get, so she could do without his outraged scorn.

She rose, smoothing the costly fabric of her clerical grey skirt over her hips. Dark grey was so slimming—so her mother maintained. It didn't seem to work on her. Edmond always managed to make her feel large. She didn't think he meant to. Jackson had made her feel almost fragile . . .

'Well, Susanna?' Edmond's neat, good-looking features carried the correct mixture of concern and censure. 'Where did you get to last night? I had an awkward few minutes trying to explain.' He sat down, crossing one impeccably creased trouser leg over the other, and she followed suit, smiling tiredly at him over the expanse of her desk, wishing her head would stop throbbing just for a moment.

'I'm sorry, Edmond,' she began, trying not to sound desperate. 'It was so hot at the Anstruthers', and I just slipped out for a moment to get some air.'

Oh, help! How much of the truth could she tell him? She had never lied to anyone, had had no reason to until now. And his face was accusing, as if he knew, as if he could see inside her head to the shameful images parading there.

Her face flooded with fiery colour as she mentally pictured how she must have looked when she'd stood the way Jackson had told her to—wantonly, shamelessly thrusting out an enormous hip, her arms upraised, large breasts bulging to the ceiling, straining against the barrier of his silky robe . . . good grief!

To banish that particularly mortifying thought she fixed her eyes with total intensity on Edmond's shiny shoes. He always bought good shoes . . . Then she flinched as he coolly intoned, 'A moment, Susanna? You didn't come back at all. I stayed on, well beyond the bounds of politeness, and had to pretend you'd made your excuses to me earlier, to pass on to her, when Lily Anstruther—who was by that time tidying up—found your handbag behind a cushion. I told her you'd developed a nasty headache. But why didn't you come back if you'd only intended to stop outside for a moment?'

Susanna was careful to keep her face composed. Edmond had once said that one of the things he most admired about her was her dignity, her composure. But inside she was a mess of wriggling misery. She would have given much to feel able to explain everything to him—the sudden restlessness, the silliness that had unaccountably possessed her, making her cast her normal caution aside, leaving her prey to the moon-madness of last night. But he would never understand. And why should he? Her behaviour had been incomprehensible. Worse than that, he would condemn her utterly, and who could blame him?

She straightened the papers on her desk and felt the sudden wetness of perspiration prickle on her back, sticking the crisp white fabric of her blouse to her skin.

'Because I wandered further than I meant to.'

There—it sounded reasonable. A few more embellishments and it would be over and done with and he would stop looking pained. *So* pained, anyway. And he would never know what had really happened, and she would make it up to him and never, ever, go off the rails again.

'I came across a wood, actually, just beyond their garden gate, and there was a stream and before I knew it I was in it. Far too wet to go back to the party. I'm sorry; there was no way I could let you know. I just had to trust to your judgment and tact to explain my absence.'

That should appease him, she thought, then frowned a little as it occurred to her that he hadn't once mentioned that he'd been worried, concerned about her whereabouts, about what might have happened to her. But before she had time to dwell on that aspect of the situation he told her acidly, making her feel quite ill again, 'My tact, as you put it, was adequate when it came to covering up for your disappearance. But even my mind boggled when Lily Anstruther phoned me this morning and said she'd found your shoes on her lawn and the jacket thing you wear with your black dress draped over a bush.'

'Oh.' She lifted shamed eyes from his shoes, her face flaming again, and sought his mild grey eyes. He still looked quite justifiably pained. 'What can I say?'

Tell him you threw odd items of clothing to the night air along with your inhibitions, an inner devil prompted slyly, but Susanna, very sane and stone-cold sober this afternoon, squashed it flat.

'Not a lot, I suppose. It's just not like you to do that sort of thing, Susanna.' He sighed heavily, shooting his cuff to enquire the time of his wrist watch. 'I must go. I've had a hectic day, and I'm due to see a client at four-thirty.' He stood up, straightening his straight tie. 'I told Lily we'd pick your things up this evening. You can smooth things

over with her then. How about if I come over to
the cottage at five-thirtyish, say? I could have a
bite of supper with you and then we could go on to
the Anstruthers'.'

'No.' She simply couldn't face up to any of it.
'I'll be working late,' she lied. 'I've got the chaps
from the inspectorate in for the next few days,
checking security, auditing accounts. And my
holiday's coming up at the beginning of next week.
I simply can't spare the time this evening.'

She couldn't spare the time, but she would. All
she could think of was the peace and quiet of her
own well-ordered little home, a soothing warm
bath and a nice hot cup of tea and some aspirins.
An evening with Edmond, no matter how decent
he was being about last night's ill-mannered,
inconsiderate behaviour on her part, plus the effort
of parrying Lily Anstruther's questions, wasn't to
be contemplated. She would make it all up to
everyone, poor Edmond particularly, some other
time.

'Oh well, work does come first; I do understand
that.' If Edmond was disappointed he didn't show
it. 'I'll fetch your things myself and smooth things
over again,' he offered, his hand on the polished
brass door knob. 'Your handbag's in my car; you're
not in a tearing hurry for it, are you?'

She shook her head, trying not to wince, glad
that the humiliating interview was over. She didn't
want to see her shoes, jacket or evening bag ever
again. They would only remind her of last night,
and she needed to forget, because if she didn't
expunge it from her mind she would spend the
next decade being ashamed of herself, wondering
exactly what had happened between him unlocking

her door and her waking up this morning in a very rumpled bed, wearing nothing at all.

Susanna always walked the short distance between the bank and her new home, one of a row of four terraced Tudor cottages, tastefully restored, that had, in the days of the small Charter town's beginnings, been almshouses. Her car, which she rarely used except for visiting her parents, was kept garaged in one of Barnham's outbuildings.

The narrow High Street was practically deserted at four-thirty that afternoon, and Susanna crossed over to the shady side, the hot June sun not improving her wretched headache. But a long, peaceful evening stretched lazily ahead of her, which was a very consoling thought. Tomorrow, surely, she would be back to being her usual capable, briskly sensible self again, last night's traumatic happenings receding in her mind, on the way to becoming forgotten. If only she could remember exactly what had happened . . .

'How are you feeling today, Susanna? Headachy?'

He had appeared from nowhere, falling in step beside her as she passed the medieval guildhall, and she stopped for one second, shattered, then marched staunchly on again, her mouth a tightly clamped line, her face flaming with a fine mixture of mortification, rage and embarrassment.

'I've been waiting, hoping I'd catch you as you left work,' he told her, his tone relaxed and outgoing, as if she'd greeted him like a long lost soul-mate instead of ignoring him, she thought crossly. 'I did wonder whether to enter the hallowed portals and ask to see you, but I reckoned I'd need more time than you'd have wanted to spare me.'

The cheek of the monster! Susanna's face turned

rodder If he had come to the bank looking like
that, asking to see her, he would have been politely
shown the door—she'd have seen to that!

Her eyes slanted sideways with outraged dismissal.
He was wearing the same tight-fitting clothes he'd
worn the night before. They'd seemed shabby last
night, by lamplight, but in the full glare of daylight
they looked disgusting! Grey frayed denims covered
with a greyish film of—what? Dust? She wrinkled
her straight nose fastidiously. Grey shirt, minus
buttons, covered with the same dust.

She averted her eyes hurriedly from the intriguing
expanse of tanned chest, muscular and coated with
crisp golden hair, as something nameless leapt
inside her, making her catch her breath.

'You look different today.' She could *hear* him
grinning, *feel* his eyes sweeping over her, *touching*.
'I guess you're wearing your lady bank manager's
hat. I prefer you the way you were last night.'

She slammed to a halt then, appalled by the
confident intimacy of his voice. She had to shake
him off. He had seen a side of her she hadn't
known existed. A side which shamed her—viewing
it from the position of the stone-cold sober. She
almost hated him for that, for seeing her the worse
for drink, wandering about in a stream, babbling
senselessly to him about her dull, dull life. And if
he thought that last night's little . . . aberration . . .
gave him the right to pester her in broad daylight,
in the middle of the High Street, then he was very
much mistaken! This was a small town, inhabitants
6,074, and everyone knew everyone, and if word
got back to Edmond that she'd been seen with this
disreputable tramp—hippie—whatever—she'd find
herself with an awful lot of explaining to do!

'Mr Arne——' He was still eating her with his

eyes, damn him! Taking in every detail from her flat grey suede shoes, her neat grey skirt, white blouse . . .

His eyes hovered on the full uptilt of her breasts, lingered on the quivering line of her soft pink mouth, then locked questioningly with hers.

'Yes, Susanna?'

In daylight his eyes were ice-green, but far from cold. Fringed with heavy, dark lashes, they danced in outrageous laughter. Peter Pan eyes in rugged, irresistibly attractive, undeniably adult-male features.

Sunlight touched the wayward lock of honey-coloured hair which fell over his wide, tanned forehead, brightening it to finest, purest gold.

She had forgotten what she'd been about to say. There was a treacherous melting, a soft warm feeling creeping all over her. It addled her brain and kept her eyes fixed on his as if there were a message to be read, somewhere in those smiling depths—if only she could understand it . . .

But this was ridiculous! Last night had been a terrible mistake, a completely out-of-character aberration, and she must get rid of him at once, make him see that she wanted nothing more to do with him.

With a monumental effort she pulled herself together, recalling one of her mother's favourite axioms. How often had Susanna heard the words 'I'm being cruel to be kind, dear' when something hurtful had been said? It was best to leave this young man—young? Thirty-fiveish, she supposed— in no doubt of the folly of his trying to presume on her regrettable lapse of the night before. She drew in a deep breath.

'Mr Arne, we have nothing to say to each other.

I'm ashamed to say that I was—well—a little under the weather when we met in the woods last night. Otherwise I wouldn't have dreamed of going to your—your house.'

'But I have a great deal to say to you, Susanna,' he butted in smoothly, his thumbs in the pockets of his jeans, the dusty fabric stretched tightly across his narrow hips, his slightly straddle-legged position underlining primitive masculine domination, his far superior height and breadth endorsing this.

Susanna fought desperately against the sheer and unaccustomed enjoyment of feeling small and fragile and feminine. She wasn't small and fragile, she told herself tartly. Facts were facts. He just had the knack of making her feel that way. Summoning all her considerable dignity, she intoned coolly, 'I deeply regret what happened last night——'

'Do you now?' Once again he cut in, preventing her from finishing what she had to say to him, and she quelled the hot tide of anger that almost had her stamping her feet in rage, and turned very cold indeed as his sleepy warm voice deflated her utterly. 'And what *did* happen last night? You don't know, do you, sweet? You might take a good guess and come up with the right answer, but you can't be sure.'

'You . . . You foul . . .'

'Hey, cool it, little lady!' He held up one large strong hand, grinning down at her, his teeth very white against his tan. 'I could give you a blow-by-blow account of exactly what happened. I was there, very much so, and I didn't pass out, believe me!'

Thick lashes dropped, shadowing hazel eyes that had darkened to agate as her body drowned in hot, embarrassed colour. She had blushed more during the past eighteen hours than she had done during the rest of her entire life, she agonised.

'Then tell me, please, Mr Arne.' She forced the words out with difficulty, her voice thick and husky. She didn't want to have to talk to this man at all, much less ask such a painfully humiliating question of him, but she owed it to herself and Edmond to find out what had happened after she'd passed out last night, and this man was the only person who could tell her.

'Jackson. The name's Jackson, remember?'

His voice prodded her, making her squirm with annoyance, but she had to go along with him for the few moments it would take to get the information from him. She muttered through a patently forced smile, 'Please tell me, Jackson.'

'That's more like it.' A hand that was incredibly gentle, despite its size and strength, tilted her chin, forcing her to meet his wickedly laughing green eyes. 'I will tell you everything, if and when you agree to listen to what I have to ask of you, and if and when you agree to agree to it. Okay?'

'That's blackmail!' she heard her voice wail. Why was she wailing? More to the point, why was she just standing here, in full view of anyone who might happen along, allowing him to touch her, to blackmail her? She didn't want to listen to what he had to ask of her, and she wouldn't agree to one damn thing!

She sought for a firmer tone, cleared her throat and found it. 'I don't care enough about what happened to allow myself to be blackmailed. All I care about is making sure it doesn't happen again.'

'And would Edmond—that is his name, isn't it?—feel the same?'

In the stunned silence that followed that carelessly
veiled threat, Susanna contemplated several things.
Falling to the pavement in a dead faint—that
seemed quite a possibility. Screaming for the
police—but they were never around when one
wanted them. Confessing all to Edmond—thereby
spiking this horrible man's guns. But what, exactly,
would she confess to?

'Think it over, sweet. I'll come and talk to you
when you're in a better state to listen to reason,'
he soothed patronisingly. 'I guess you're still feeling
groggy after last night's debauchery. Already drunk
when I came across you in the woods? And the
best part of a bottle of wine after that. Tsk! Tsk!'
He shook his tousled blond head slowly, his eyes
piously lifted, and Susanna could have hit him, she
really could; only a supreme effort of will prevented
her doing just that!

And then the moment of danger was past,
because he gave her a grinning, 'See you, Susanna,'
and loped away, his long, easy strides carrying him
down the street.

She had a scant quarter of a mile to walk before
she reached the sanctuary of her home. She
stamped past the last of the shops, past the straggle
of new houses, Barnham's farmyard and the
paddock where the Barnham's pony grazed at full
throttle, growing hotter and crosser by the second,
snorting from time to time, startling old Mr Potts,
her next-door neighbour who was mulching roses
in his front garden.

She didn't calm down until she'd bathed, changed
into a navy cotton shirtwaister and swallowed
several cups of tea and three aspirins. By then
she'd run out of steam, and the outraged anger

had burned itself out, leaving a nagging, niggling chord of anxiety twanging in her mind.

What *had* happened last night? Quite a lot, if Jackson Arne's implications were anything to go by. He could be stringing her along, of course, turning the screw, but he had blatantly told her that he wanted her. So had he taken her?

The thought of it made her burn all over with a sensation that wasn't entirely shame, she realised, mortified by her body's instinctive reaction to the erotic pictures that presented themselves in her startled brain, by the hussy-like regret that she would never be able to recall exactly how it felt to be made love to by Jackson Arne.

But surely to goodness she would know if she were no longer a virgin?

Susanna gnawed at her lower lip, her stomach clenching into knots as she stepped out of her neat, newly furnished sitting-room and into her front garden.

Hers was the end cottage, and there was a narrow green lane which was just wide enough to take a tractor running at the side of her garden, past the four cottage gardens at the back, debouching into the fields, by way of a gate, where Jackson was squatting in a hovel. That much she could remember of last night.

She sank wearily into the canvas chair in the porch and closed her eyes, listening to the distant call of a cuckoo, the closer buzz of a bee in the sun-warmed flowers. Somehow she had to find out what had happened after she'd passed out. If she recalled the preceding events carefully, she might remember something. So, slowly, she re-lived what had happened after he'd said he wanted her and pulled her to her feet, into his arms.

He'd said, 'Come on, Susanna,' his arms holding her, his hands gentling her. 'I'll take you home.'

She had murmured something against his chest, muzzy words about missing shoes, and one of his hands had carefully pushed a swathe of hair back from her face, his head coming down, his lips tender as he placed a lightly reassuring kiss on her flushed cheek. 'Don't worry about a thing. You'll be fine. Just fine.' He had swept her up into his arms, carrying her as if she were made of thistledown, pushing the door open with his foot.

It was like something out of an old fairytale, Susanna had thought, snuggling closer into his warmth, her head resting gratefully against his broad chest, his male scent in her nostrils, her arms twined shamelessly around his neck.

Somewhere an owl had called, and night creatures had rustled in the shaggy hedgerows, and the moon had shone behind the deep amethyst veil of mist; the long grass had whispered as his bare feet passed.

He had no longer seemed frightening and menacing. He was taking care of her, taking her home, and it had all been quite deliciously unlike anything that had ever happened to her before. It was the sort of thing that happened to beautiful, slender blondes— not to big, plain, boring females like S. Bryce-Jones! And he had had to be incredibly strong to be able to carry her at all, and he hadn't even been out of breath as he murmured, 'Mallow Cottage, didn't you say? It's only a stone's throw over the meadow—the lane runs right behind the gardens and at the side of your house.'

And in a disappointingly short space of time he had deposited her gently in the porch, steadying her with one hand as he asked, 'The door key?'

Susanna had shaken her head very slowly, giggling. 'Lost. In my bag. Lost at Lily's.'

'I see.'

He hadn't grumbled, as Edmond would have done, and she had been glad of that because now she was no longer safely held in his arms, she was back to feeling peculiar again—and not at all fit to be grumbled at.

He had been already moving round the outside of the cottage, looking for open windows, when she had remembered. She'd tottered after him, clutching at the robe of his she still wore.

'There's a spare key—under——' She had waved one arm haphazardly, direction unknown, and he'd steered her gently back to the porch.

'Where do you keep the spare key, sweet? Tell me.'

And she remembered trying to say 'Under the pot with the nasturtiums in it,' without slurring her words too disgracefully. And she remembered giggling again and sliding slowly down the door frame. And then nothing. Nothing at all. Try as she might, she could recall nothing between that and waking this morning. Nude.

Had he unlocked the door, bundled her inside, and left her to it? She didn't think so. The state she'd been in she wouldn't have been able to get up the stairs, let alone get undressed and into bed. And there'd been no sign of the wretched man's robe anywhere around this morning, and she'd checked again after she'd had her bath this evening. So he must have taken it with him when he'd left. Stripped her bra and pants off, too. Then put her to bed. Alone?

The very thought of his hands stripping her naked, never mind anything else, brought her bounding up

out of the chair, her face contorted as she struggled
with outrage, shame and despair.

'What *is* the matter, dear? You look horribly
ferocious!'

Susanna hadn't heard her mother's car draw up,
nor the snicking sound the latch of the garden gate
made. But Miranda Bryce-Jones was standing on the
path, her slender self as elegant as ever in a polka
dot silk suit in brown and cream, her smooth auburn
hair artfully styled, her cornflower blue eyes slightly
cynical as she regarded her large, cross offspring.

'Lily Anstruther phoned to tell me you'd been
unwell. So I dropped by on my way to bridge with
the Clooneys to see for myself.' Miranda moved
gracefully up the path, past Susanna, and into the
cottage. 'I can't stay, dear; I've got to re-track a
good ten miles, but I could make time for a nice
cold G and T, if you've got such a thing.'

Miranda sank down on a chintz-covered armchair,
and Susanna hovered, feeling huge. She always felt
huger and clumsier than usual when faced with her
mother's five-four slender loveliness.

'Yes, of course,' she mumbled, horrified to learn
that Lily had obviously been tattling all over the
county. Before last night Susanna hadn't been invited
to one of Lily's evening affairs. For one thing, she'd
been living and studying and, later, working in
London, and for the first few months of her time at
the Much Barton branch she'd been living with her
parents. Her parents had been, on a few occasions;
that went without saying because Miranda and Trevor
Bryce-Jones were high in the county hierachy and an
Asset. And last night, as Edmond had put it, he and
Susanna had Arrived, been Accepted into the upper
echelons, as it were, of the small-town community.
And Susanna, first off, had blown it! Not that such

social jockeying interested her, but it interested Edmond.

'Well, dear?' One of Miranda's arched eyebrows rose pointedly, and Susanna pulled herself together and rushed out to the kitchen to fix the drink. The very sight of the gin bottle made her feel queasy. She never drank it herself, hating the taste, but she kept it for Edmond and for her mother's visitations.

The ice cubes were chattering in the glass as Susanna carried it through, an audible translation of the way her hands were shaking, and Miranda, accepting it, said with a frosty smile, 'Lily tells me you left various items of clothing positively *strewn* all over her nice garden, dear. I told her that if that were the case then you had quite obviously been taken ill and that she'd been right to phone me. " Lily, dear thing," I said to her, "my daughter has, if nothing else, the constitution of an ox. She is never unwell unless she has eaten something disagreeable." I thought that put her in her place quite well, don't you, dear? She serves some atrocious rubbish at those parties of hers, as I know from experience. Now, why don't you tell me your version of what happened? Surely you weren't crass enough to duck out, leaving all manner of sundry garments draped all over those vulgar azaleas she's always gushing on about?'

'I did not!' snapped Susanna, aggrieved. Like Edmond, her mother had shown no concern about the possible state of her health. She could really have been ill, have been dying down there in the azaleas, and they would only have cared about how it would have looked. Appearances were everything.

Seeing Miranda's look of icy surprise at having been spoken to so sharply, Susanna was immediately ashamed. She was feeling rather frayed around the edges by now, possibly over-reacting, and, unlike her father, her mother had always taken an interest in her, been kind, according to her lights.

'Sorry,' she sighed, dropping into an armchair which was a twin of the one her mother was using. 'I didn't mean to snap. I left my shoes there and that bolero thing. It was too tight under the arms and the night was so hot.'

'Too tight? I thought the outfit looked rather well on you. But maybe we should have settled for the midnight blue with the chiffon sleeves, after all. At least you wouldn't have been able to strew bits of that around the place,' Miranda commented wryly, finishing her drink and putting the empty glass on a small side table. 'You'd better tell me your version of what happened after you'd done your partial strip-tease, hadn't you? Forewarned is forearmed, as they say.'

Sighing, feeling drained and queasy again, Susanna repeated what she'd said to Edmond and added the rider that she hoped the whole thing would blow over soon, and Miranda, giving her a very funny look, said, 'So do I dear, so do I. Tell me one thing more—and then I simply must fly—what did Lily give you to drink?'

Susanna struggled to her feet as her mother stood up, settling her cream-coloured leather handbag under her arm. The subject of drink wasn't an appealing one.

'Wine. Red or white. It was ready-poured—glasses of the stuff here and there. One helped oneself.'

'I see. It was probably very inferior plonk. Which would account for your sudden indisposition, together with the dubious eatables. I shall mention the wine, in passing, when I next speak to Lily. That should quieten her tongue.' Miranda bestowed a brilliant smile on her quailing daughter and glided to the front door. 'Lily wouldn't want the doubtful nature of the refreshments she offers bruited around, would she, dear?'

The smile was charmingly assured now. All was, if not forgotten, forgiven, Susanna supposed. She was uneasy about her mother's methods, but she knew from past experience that nothing she said would alter Miranda's decision, once taken. Her mother would ever-so-sweetly lay the blame for Susanna's suspect behaviour on poor Lily's food and drink. She bent her head to receive her mother's vague kiss of farewell and automatically reached to open the door. And the breath was sucked out of her body, as if she'd received a blow to the body, because Jackson Arne was standing on the doorstep, practically blocking out the daylight with his impressive frame.

He stepped over the threshold, looming over Susanna, completely dwarfing Miranda, and Susanna had just enough time to think, he's up to no good, before he held out her rumpled black dress, suspending it by two long forefingers from the narrow straps so that it couldn't possibly be mistaken for what it was.

'I came to return this, sweet. You left it on my sitting-room floor last night.'

His face was perfectly straight but his eyes were dancing, glinting with wicked emerald lights, and Susanna's mouth went dry and she wanted to scream and go on screaming until some kind soul took pity on her and removed her gently to a peaceful place, away from the horrible nightmare her life had suddenly become.

CHAPTER THREE

'SUSANNA, will you walk with me to my car?'

Her mother's voice washed over her like a shower of icy water, and after glaring at Jackson and receiving an unashamed grin for her trouble, Susanna rushed down the garden path after Miranda's dignified, retreating figure.

'Who is that man?'

'Er—Jackson Arne.'

'And what was he doing with your dress? The dress you wore to Lily's party last night? And what was it doing on his sitting-room floor? No, don't tell me; I don't want to know!' Miranda was furious—it showed in the white circle around her pinched mouth, in the cold sparks of rage in the cornflower-blue eyes.

'I could explain,' Susanna hissed tersely, one part of her mind concentrating on the likelihood of that hateful man standing on her doorstep, avidly eavesdropping on the row he'd so odiously instigated.

'I don't want you to. I don't want to hear the disgusting details of your sordid sex life. My mind is boggling enough as it is. But get rid of him. Now!'

High heels clicked an agitated tattoo over the pavement to the car parked at the kerb. Extracting a key ring from her handbag, Miranda ground out,

'I repeat—get rid of him. Permanently. If Edmond gets to hear of this little peccadillo he'll call the wedding off. And if that happens he'll make sure everyone knows the reason way. And in that event, daughter dear, not even I will be able to lay a thick enough smokescreen. You will be the laughing stock of the entire neighbourhood, a legitimate target for endless gossip—not to mention jokes of the lewder kind. Your position at the bank will become untenable.'

As she listened to the receding roar of her mother's car, Susanna blinked back scalding tears. Every word Miranda had said was true. All her present misery, even down to the hammer which was pounding away inside her head again, could be laid at the feet of that obnoxious man!

He was somewhere in there, inside the house. She didn't want to have to face him because she knew she was capable of strangling him, big as he was, in the murderous mood she was in right now!

But he had to be faced, and the only way out of her present impossible situation was to get the truth regarding last night out of him. Even if it meant she had to listen to whatever it was he had to ask of her, she had to do it because not knowing how dreadfully she'd behaved was driving her out of her mind.

She walked up the path slowly, lingering in the porch, trying to calm a mind which was skittering out of control like a brain-damaged gnat. Once she had the truth, she would know how to act. If Jackson had done nothing worse to her than put her to bed she would tell Edmond all there was to know about the whole miserable affair. He was a fair-minded man, balanced and rational; he would be angry, and she wouldn't blame him, but he

would at least be able to see last night's folly for
what it was: a regrettable lapse, cause unknown,
which would never be repeated.

And if Jackson Arne had taken advantage of her
inebriated condition, she would have to return
Edmond's ring and tell him she'd had second
thoughts. Her mother would not be pleased.

Squaring her shoulders, she walked into the
house, seeking him, determined to conduct the
coming humiliating interview with dignity. She
found him in her kitchen, casually perched on one
of the tall pine stools, the wretched black dress
draped over another.

My, but he looks pleased with himself, she
thought with a surge of temper, holding on to
herself with difficulty. She had to box clever, play
it cool, not give way to the need to throw the
nearest heavy object at his head. She'd get the
truth out of him—then let him have it, wouldn't
she just!

Beneath discreetly lowered lashes she weighed
him up. Unfairly attractive he might be, but he
was also feckless. No man who went around dressed
like that, who acted the way he did, who said the
things he said, could be anything but.

There was always a solution to every problem.
Long years of hard training had taught her that,
taught her to take the logical viewpoint. There was
no point in railing at him like a fishwife; the
situation had gone far beyond that. And the idea
of appealing to his better nature, of telling him
that he was set fair to ruining her life, never mind
her reputation, if he didn't leave her alone and get
out of her life as suddenly as he'd entered it, was a
non-starter. If Jackson Arne wanted something he
went right ahead and grabbed it, no matter who

got ground under his heels in the process. That much, if nothing else, she had learned about him. And he did want something of her; he'd said as much.

She looked him full in the face, saw the amused curl of his wide male mouth, and swung her eyes away quickly, her heart pattering erratically.

He had a strange effect on her, but she was too sensible, basically, anyway—last night didn't count—to allow a little thing like that to budge her from her firm intention to have the truth from him and then clear him out of her life.

'Very well, Mr Arne, you've had your fun. You've persuaded my mother that I'm some sort of loose woman, so let's dispense with the practical jokes, shall we, and get down to business?'

'Your mother?' Dark brown eyebrows hunched. 'You're not a bit alike.'

'That's irrelevant.' She didn't need reminding that she bore about as much resemblance to her gracefully elegant mother as did a Great Dane to a French Poodle.

'Would you say so?' Astute green eyes held hers soberly for one heart-stopping moment before his lazy grin took over, the eyes—now darkening with intimacy—sliding over her in a look that seemed to burn through the prim shirtwaister to the flesh beneath. 'I'd say she excelled herself when she produced a masterpiece like you.'

The sheer sarcastic effrontery of that remark successfully iced down the surging heat that had flooded unstoppably through her, raging in full spate wherever his eyes had touched her. It was one thing to listen to, and partially believe, such blatant untruths in a moon-filled woodland setting, with wine coursing insidiously through her veins.

Another thing altogether to listen to such lies in the full glare of daylight, in her neatly practical kitchen.

'I asked you to forget the jokes,' she growled, and Jackson whispered silkily,

'Who's joking? And believe me, I didn't know anyone would be here when I returned your dress, let alone your mother.' The small crinkles around his eyes deepened. 'I thought I ought to bring it back. For all I knew you might need it to wear if you intend going out on the razzle again tonight.'

Susanna met that piece of rudeness with the contempt it deserved. Disdainful hazel met wickedly smiling ice-green in a long haughty stare that began to falter when his mouth twitched, curving one-sidedly in a mocking smile that touched a chord deep inside her, making her own lips relax, soften, quiver, as she wondered bemusedly what that mouth would feel like, covering hers.

'I don't go out on the razzle, as you so crudely put it.' Her voice came out sounding throaty, not clipped and incisive as she'd intended, and it ruined the impact of her statement, almost making it sound wistful, and he must have picked it up because he taunted,

'Are you telling me that last night was the first time for you?'

The sexual innuendo, the horror of not knowing, scorched her cheeks, and she snatched up the now-hated black dress from the stool, wrinkling her nose at the pond-weed smell that clung to the fabric.

'The first, the last and the only!' she groaned, lifting bewildered eyes to his, then quickly turning away to hide the sudden and shattering sensation of vulnerability that made her tremble. She mustn't reveal a trace of weakness in front of him!

Hurriedly, hardly knowing what she was doing, she stuffed the dress into the kitchen waste bin, seeing the chromium-plated lid snap back, hiding the shame-making object from view. She never wanted to see—much less wear—the thing again!

'You are in a state, aren't you?' Jackson's voice came from right behind her, warm and soothing, and she stiffened, snapping,

'Can you blame me!'

'I don't know, yet.' Two strong yet gentle hands fell on her shoulders, their pressure insidious, easing her backwards until her body touched his. Rigid, unable to draw a breath, she strove to ignore the curling sensation of heat, the quicksilver shooting of fire that squirrelled around deep in her stomach.

'When we met this afternoon I couldn't read you at all, not after the way you were last night. But I think I'm beginning to get the picture now.'

His voice had the quality of a well-practised caress, and his hands, seductive, infinitely persuasive on her shoulders, began to knead and soothe, gentling the tension away, moving subtly to the base of her neck, long supple fingers stroking, sliding down to the hollows below her collarbone, stopping just short of the soft, fully rounded upper curves of her breasts.

She knew she should move away, tell him to keep his hands to himself, but she seemed rooted to the spot, dumb and witless!

'Relax, Susanna. Relax.' His moulding hands moved lower, just a fraction, teasing, and her breasts hardened, aching, seeming to thrust with an open invitation for more, much more.

'You're much too uptight, sweet.' The balls of his thumbs stroked the nape of her neck. 'There, that's better, isn't it? Just let go. Feel good.'

The words were whispered slowly, his breath touching the skin of her neck, his lips close, so close. Shuddering, in the grip of something totally new to her, she heard his voice deepen roughly. 'I just hate to think of the lovely lady I met last night never being let out of that female bank manager prison you seem to be trying to confine her in.' His hands caressed, and his hard hips pressured the softness of her buttocks, and her eyes flew open as she fought the crazy thing that was telling her to turn in his arms, lift her eager mouth to his.

This *was* crazy! He was a threat and she knew it, menacing her well-ordered existence, the composed self-image that had been painstakingly built up, brick by brick, the total control she had always had over her body. To allow him to touch her, get near her at all, was madness. Last night she had indulged in enough madness to last a lifetime!

'Take your hands off me!'

'Sure.' His hands immediately snapped back to his sides and his wide shoulders lifted in a careless shrug. 'So the lady enjoys feeling tense and uptight.' He met stormy hazel eyes that slid away, quickly veiled beneath the heavy lashes that swept flushed cheeks. 'How about a coffee? I'll make it.'

There was no fazing him, Susanna fumed inwardly as he moved away on quiet, rope-soled feet, and she watched with unconcealed hostility as he filled the electric kettle and plugged it in, searching through her cupboards for mugs and coffee granules.

'Make yourself at home, why don't you?'

'Thanks.' There was a grin in his voice. 'That's

what I like to hear—open-handed hospitality from a beautiful woman.'

He had chosen to ignore her sarcasm, but she couldn't ignore his. Beautiful woman, indeed! She was very far from being that. She knew it, everyone knew it, and his cruelty hurt.

And to her utter chagrin—because she never cried—her eyes filled with scalding tears, spilling over, and Jackson turned with steaming mugs in his hands, a frown line appearing between his eyes.

He put the mugs down on the counter and moved towards her, concerned compassion darkening his eyes to winter evergreen. Guessing his intention, she hurriedly backed off. She couldn't take any more of his comforting, his glib philosophising.

'We may as well drink that outside, as you've made it.' She twirled round, moving swiftly. Outside the kitchen door there was a small paved area, four white-painted cast iron chairs and one table. It overlooked a small lawn surrounded by freshly dug, straight-sided borders which were empty of plants because she hadn't got around to buying them yet.

Slumping heavily down on one of the chairs, she stared with clouded eyes over the garden, past the low hedge along the bottom, the higher field hedge on the other side of the green lane, the woods on the far side of the meadow where she and Jackson had emerged last night into moonlight and mist.

Biting her lips in exasperation, she turned jerkily as he walked towards her, carrying the two mugs, and the air was suddenly charged with his electric virility, and the tension between them.

Nothing was going as she had planned it to. By now she should have had the truth about what had actually happened last night out of him, and should

have sent him on his way, if not ashamed of
himself, then at least knowing that he'd met his
match, that his presence in her life was not wanted,
his attempts at blackmail a joke, a waste of time.

Instead, he had taken over, directed her every
word and action, reduced her to a quivering mass
of lustful desires, opened her eyes to an inner
sexuality she hadn't known she possessed, reduced
her to tears.

It had to stop. Right now. Fixing him with a
basilisk stare as he took the chair opposite hers,
ignoring the mug he'd put down on the table in
front of her, she asked icily, 'So what happened
last night after I passed out?' spoiling the effect of
her businesslike tone by blushing furiously as a
slow, sensuous, reminiscent smile gave his rugged
features the fleeting look of a pagan satyr.

'I carried you upstairs and put you to bed,' he
answered easily.

And took my clothes off! her mind screeched.
And as if picking the thought out of her mind, he
grinned. 'Don't look so shocked, sweet; there's
nothing to be ashamed of in a beautiful body.'

This time she didn't let his cruelty hurt. Thinning
her mouth, her knuckles clenching on the arm rests
of her chair, she rasped, 'And then what?'

'You don't remember? You really don't? So
much for the women who've told me I'm
unforgettable!' Disbelief blanked his face before
his features assumed a parodied mask of hurt
feelings, and she knew it was all an outrageous act
to tighten the screw, to bring her nerves to
screaming pitch again.

'So tell me. It's important.'

'How important, sweet?'

'Don't call me that!'

'Why not? Aren't you?'

'Oh!' Exasperation snatched the breath from her throat. She had to get away from him, she had to find a space where she could breathe in peace! 'Get lost!' she snapped, stumbling to her feet, fury throbbing in her temples.

She was setting new records for losing her temper. Since meeting this vile joker, who obviously couldn't take anything seriously, not even the vexed question of her virtue, she had done little else— she, who was well known, and prided herself on it, for being one of the most equable creatures alive!

A strong hand snaked out as she tried to push past him, snaring her wrist, the pressure the hard fingers exerted forcing her down on to the chair again. Still holding her wrist, he leaned across the table, his eyes suddenly serious and frightening in his strong face.

'How important, Susanna?' His fingers tightened fractionally, making her wince. 'Tell me how important it is to you and then I'll tell you why it's important to me.'

He was calling all the tunes, and she was beyond fighting him on this. Scowling, her eyes stormy, she told him, 'Because I'm getting married at Christmas, so figure it out for yourself!'

'Ah, yes. Edmond, of course.' Ice-green eyes slid down to the narrow hoop of diamonds and he released her wrist, one finger moving over the glittering stones with a dismissive brevity that amounted to mockery. 'And Edmond would be far from happy if he got to hear about last night's little indiscretion. Especially if——' he shrugged, the slight movement provocative, and Susanna's eyes dropped, shying away from what she read in his, lingering on the open V of his shirt, the tanned skin, hard muscles, crisp golden hair, held by a fascination that was stronger than her will.

He lifted his mug, sipping, his sleepy eyes irresistibly drawing hers back to meet his teasing look.

'I understand your predicament, sweet, and I hope you'll try to understand mine. Will you try?'

She nodded resignedly. Now for the crunch. His predicament would probably amount to an acute lack of funds. Her stupid behaviour had made her the ideal target for blackmail. She had no one to blame but herself.

'I tried to put it to you last night, but you were—indisposed, shall we say? So I'll try again. I will tell you, detail for delicious detail, exactly what happened after I'd finished undressing you, if you'll agree to pose for me.'

His hand crept across the table, ensnaring hers, tightening so that Edmond's ring bit into her flesh, making her grit her teeth with the pain of it, with the deeper pain of knowing what the metal and stone signified.

Surprised, because this was the last thing she'd expected to have him ask, Susanna croaked, 'Pose? Pose for what?' and he grinned widely, letting go of her hand, only to reach out and run his fingers over her cheek.

'I'm a sculptor by trade, sweet. A carver of stone with a commission—a big one. Before last night I hadn't a single idea worth giving house room to, because normally I choose my own subjects, do my own thing. And then I saw you, walking through the moonlight in the water, and ideas clicked so rapidly it was like seeing the stone take shape in front of me. And by the time you were ready to leave the cottage I knew I wanted you, had to have you. You'd make the perfect model.'

It all clicked into place then. The greyish dust on his clothes. His working clothes. The intent, absorbed way he looked at her. The quality of stillness, of watchfulness last night as he'd got her to do the talking, left her to prattle on, her tongue wine-loosened, not listening to what she was saying but weighing up her possibilities, her potential as a model. And that was why he had touched her, last night in the wood.

And the thing that hurt, made her feel cold inside with the shame of knowing that it hurt, was the realisation that although he'd called her 'Magnificent' and 'Superb', said that he wanted her, he hadn't been meaning that he'd wanted her as a man wants a desirable woman, but as a suitable study for some stone effigy.

'The perfect model for what?' she grated, hoping her humiliation didn't show. 'An all-in female wrestler?' And instead of laughing, as she'd expected him to, he frowned, the lines cutting into his forehead, darkening his eyes.

'Don't put yourself down. It must be a deep-seated habit with you—you do it with so much conviction. Will you pose for me? I promise it won't take up too much of your time. I'll only need you for the initial drawings. A couple of sessions of, say, three hours apiece.'

'No.'

He didn't threaten her now; only her own senseless reaction to him did that. To see him again, to pose for him, give him the time he needed to make his drawings, would be to deepen her disastrous vulnerability to him, lay herself open to emotions she didn't want to know about. Dared not know about.

She knew now that all he had done last night was to heave an inert body upstairs and put it to bed. He wouldn't have made love to her. He hadn't wanted her at all, or only as a possible model for some monstrous statue. He didn't see her as a woman. Only as a shape in a lump of stone. Nothing had happened last night. She was very sure about that.

'Are you certain you want to say no, Susanna?'

His soft question startled her, jolting her out of her thoughts, and her eyes swept over him, possibly for the last time, and she said the first inconsequential thing that came into her head. 'I thought it was dirt. Grime. That you never bothered to wash your clothes.'

'Stone dust—I get smothered in it. It's an occupational hazard.'

He followed the direction of her thoughts in the alarming way he had and his mouth hardened. 'I'm not one of the great unwashed, so I won't have sullied you. I've been hacking away at an abstract for my own satisfaction, trying to clear my mind for the commissioned piece. But you did it for me.'

He lounged back in the chair, one long denim-clad leg hooked casually over the other, sunlight gilding his rumpled honey-blond hair, touching the golden tips of the dark lashes that narrowed his eyes to glittering emerald slits.

Susanna swallowed against the hard lump of misery in her chest. Last night she had let the moonlight and wine go to her head, had listened to his sultry compliments, allowing them to beguile her, had believed the unbelievable.

Now, with the early evening sun suddenly seeming to oppress her with its weight, highlighting what she really was—a large plain woman in a dowdy sensible dress—she couldn't credit that she'd been fool enough to imagine for one moment that the ruggedly attractive man opposite, with his aura of vibrant virility, potent masculinity, could have found her desirable. The idea would be laughable, if only it didn't hurt so much.

'Are you quite sure you don't want to pose for me?' he asked again, and as she shook her head tiredly he went on with remorseless frankness. 'So you've stopped wondering about last night? You feel you can take not knowing, either way? It won't matter to you, or to Edmond, whether I made love to you or not, whether you lay with me and held me, gave yourself and enjoyed it . . .'

The mind-pictures he conjured up were unendurable. He, whose magnificent body would arouse any woman he fancied—and he would only fancy lovely, graceful women—taunting the plain woman who had never aroused any man to passion, not even Edmond who wanted to marry her, with images which sent the blood racing through her veins.

She stood up wearily, feeling a hundred years old, the reflected glare from the white-painted table top hurting her eyes. She couldn't look at him, hating him more for the cruel way he mocked her with images of the impossible than she'd hated him when she'd stupidly believed in the possibility of his having made love to her.

'It's no use your waving that threat over my head.' Her words dropped like slow heavy stones into the humid air, the line of her shoulders

showing her defeat. 'You put me to bed, and that's
all. You wouldn't have wanted me—that way.'

'Can you be so sure?'

Attuned to everything about him, she sensed the
lithe uncoiling movement that brought him to his
feet, standing over her. She shrugged as he waited
for an answer, too humiliated by her unwilling
attraction to a man who wouldn't look at her
twice, except as a possible model for a commission
he had to fulfil, to raise the energy for more verbal
fencing, then her breath caught sharply in her
throat as his fingers bit into her arms, dragging her
round to face him.

Her eyes were on a level with the base of his
throat and she could see a pulse beating heavily
beneath the firm tanned skin. He tipped his hand
under her chin, forcing her head up, holding her
eyes.

'Can you be so sure that I didn't want you from
the first moment I saw you? Can you, Susanna?
That I didn't know what heaven those voluptuous
curves would be in my bed?'

His green gaze dropped to her lips, and Susanna
felt her mouth part in mindless invitation, her legs
grow weak as the force of wanting deep inside her,
the force he had so effortlessly brought to powerful
life, gripped her with its fever-like intensity.

Shockingly aware of her weakness where he was
concerned, she desperately tried to fix her mind on
something prosaic, like the overhead telephone
wires, but her gaze was hypnotically brought back
to him, and all she could see was the sensual,
predatory curve of his beautiful male mouth, all
she could feel was the erratic beating of her heart,
the explosion of heated sensation as his hands
moved, delicately exploring the full curves of her

breasts, sliding with warm enticement down to her voluptuous hips.

'I find you a very desirable package indeed. Shall I prove it to you, sweet, beyond a shadow of doubt?' he murmured with seductive slowness while his mouth trailed soft kisses along her cheekbone and down, lingering, teasing, at the corner of her mouth.

'Can't you sense it, sweet? Feel it?' Strong male hands slid around to her back, pulling her close so that her pliant body was pressed against his hardness, and his lips took her mouth, demanding a surrender she hadn't the strength to withhold.

Her lips parted beneath the probing intentness of his, and, gone beyond sanity, she shuddered weakly as his tongue invaded the inner sweetness of her mouth in a provocative suggestion of the inevitability of what was to come, or a reminder of what was past.

Instinctively, her hands moved up, her fingers searching, finding and exploring the hollows behind his ears, fluttering on to curl into the crispness of hair at his nape.

Jackson was breathing heavily, deepening the kiss, his hands moving possessively over the soft curves of her body, leaving a fiery trail of sensation wherever they touched. Susanna groaned helplesssly as he sparked feelings she had never known before, manipulating her, demanding and getting responses she hadn't known she had to give.

She heard a deep, ragged groan rock its way through him and felt him shudder. Then, abruptly, he held her away from him, and she saw the glazed look of desire in his smoky green eyes. Her own were hazed with her body's need of him as he told her, his voice roughened, 'Now say I don't want you. Tell me I wasn't driven crazy with wanting when I helped you to get undressed, held your magnificent naked body in my arms . . . Tell me that, and you'll be lying in your teeth.'

His eyes glittered savagely as he lifted her face in fingers that were suddenly hard and cruel before he possessed her mouth with brief, brutal punishment. But the old mocking look was back as he released her again, the curling lift of his mouth in evidence as he told her lightly. 'Think it over, sweet. And don't make any mistake—I'll be back for my answer. I want you and I'm going to have you. You'll give in, in the end. See you.'

Then he was gone, striding over the lawn with loose-limbed grace, vaulting effortlessly over the boundary hedge, and Susanna was left, bewildered, frightened and almost painfully excited by what had happened to her. He did find her desirable, there had been no mistaking that, and her fingers tentatively touched her soft, bruised mouth, the mouth that had received his passion, revelled in it, returned it.

CHAPTER FOUR

EVERY Friday lunchtime Susanna and Edmond met in the bar of the Dog and Duck, had a snack lunch, and discussed their plans for Saturday and Sunday. Susanna always mildly looked forward to it; it marked the beginning of the wind-down for the weekend.

But today, as she tidied her hair prior to leaving the bank to meet him, she felt apprehensive. And that was odd.

She hadn't seen Edmond since the morning after Lily's party, three days ago, but that wasn't unusual because they were both busy people. And she hadn't seen Jackson, either, since he'd kissed her, leaving her in no doubt at all that—fantastic though it might seem—he did find her physically desirable.

Maybe his absence, after he'd told her he'd be back for his answer, was the cause of the fluttery, half-apprehensive, half-excited edginess that had taken hold of her just lately. When he'd held her, kissed her, she had known the reality of his wanting. And she had known just how easily he could make her respond to him.

And that meant that he could easily have made love to her on the night of Lily's party. She could have cheated on poor Edmond without being properly aware of it, without even remembering!

Sighing, she eyed her reflection in the washroom

mirror without enthusiasm. Her dark hair was
neatly secured in its customary severe style, her
generous figure discreetly covered in a plain
charcoal-grey cotton twill suit. She looked precisely
as she always looked, no better, no worse, so why
this sudden discontent? She had come to terms
with her image years ago and nothing had changed
except for her lips—full and slightly parted, instead
of compressed and unyieldingly firm, reminding
her of the changes wrought in her. Changes she
didn't want or need, she told herself crossly,
dropping her powder compact back into her
shoulder bag and snapping it shut.

It was all very well for a man like Jackson Arne
to come along, fill her head with his easy flattery,
fill her body with restless desires that could never
be fulfilled. He would forget her soon enough,
move on to take his ephemeral pleasures elsewhere,
and not once during their engagement had Edmond's
chaste, dry kisses moved her to more than a vague
sense of uneasiness—making her feel silly, almost.

The memory of how it had felt to be kissed by
Jackson Arne intruded hotly, and she pushed it
firmly aside. She was going to marry Edmond.
Edmond's kisses would have to be enough. The
memory of those wanton longings must be banished,
because no good could come of remembering. It
would be unfair to Edmond, unfair to herself.

Leaving the washroom, Susanna walked rapidly
down the corridor and stood in the doorway of the
main office, glancing over the heads of her
industrious staff to the front counter. It was
deserted, but she expected that, because although
counter business was always brisk on a Friday
morning it slackened to nothing from around noon.

All was peaceful and as it should be, and she

said briskly, because she felt that briskness tempered with just an inflexion of warmth was what was expected of a woman in her position, 'I'm going for lunch now; I won't be longer than three-quarters of an hour,' and thanked heaven that she was taking two weeks of her annual holiday entitlement as from this evening.

And that was another odd thing. Being sensible, she had always recognised that one needed a break from time to time in order to maintain one's highest standards during the rest of the working year. She had always looked on holidays as a duty rather than a pleasure. But now she was longing for time off, which was, she knew, another manifestation of the edgy restlessness that had possessed her since the night of Lily's party.

Edmond had secured a corner table in the busy bar, no mean feat since the Dog and Duck, largely unchanged since the days of James the First—except for a few quaint Victorian additions—was currently the in-place for the small town's business community to take lunch.

Susanna slid on to the bench seat beside him, her smile wary because she felt guilty and she didn't know whether he was still annoyed with her over her defection from the party.

But his answering smile was just the way it always was—bland. And he handed her the bar snack menu, which she perused unnecessarily because she always chose the quiche and salad and he always had the steak and kidney pie. And he had already got their drinks in: half a pint of lager and lime for him and an unsweetened orange juice for her because she was trying to be on a diet. All her life she'd been trying to diet. Uselessly.

'I'll have the quiche, please,' she said, as she

said every Friday lunchtime, and he said, 'Steak and kidney for me, I think,' which was what he always said, too.

Susanna watched him push his way through to the bar with their orders and wondered why they had sunk into such a rut after only eight months of knowing each other and ten weeks of being engaged. Already they seemed like an old married couple. Incredibly old, now she came to think of it. There were no surprises, no excitement.

But that didn't bother her, did it? It shouldn't. It never had done before. A well-ordered life, which was what they both wanted, didn't contain excitement or surprises. Excitement was a disruptive element, and surprises could be unpleasant as well as not.

When his thigh brushed hers as he slid back on to the bench seat Susanna felt nothing. Not even the smallest tingle. And just to make sure, she took his hand—which at least would give him a surprise because he wasn't a physical man and had a horror of public displays of any kind. But beyond noting that his hand felt clammy because he must be stifling in his business suit and very correctly tied tie, she felt no sensation whatsoever.

Remembering the dizzy, melting, aching feeling that had swept through her entire body when Jackson touched her, Susanna was consumed by guilt. She removed her hand from Edmond's passive clasp and scrabbled in her capacious handbag to cover her confusion and hide the hot, shameful flush that always afflicted her when she thought about Jackson Arne.

Then, as if her mind had conjured him up, he was there, shouldering his way through the tight knots of lunchtime customers, a good head taller and broader by far than any other male in sight.

Her stomach clenched sickeningly as, inevitably, he came to their table, as if he had been able to sense her out in the crowd. He was smiling his outrageous smile and her legs went weak, just looking at him, and she was glad she was sitting down because if she hadn't been she might have fallen.

As ever, he was casually dressed. His black shirt, though at least clean and free of the patina of stone dust, was left unbuttoned, affording her wide, apprehensive eyes a pulse-quickening glimpse of his muscular, tanned chest.

Her eyes dropped quickly, denying the temptation to stare, then shied away, blinking, from the devastating sight of cream-coloured denims gripping hard male thighs.

'Morning, Susanna.'

His smile encompassed her, folded her into its warmth, heating her blood yet sending a shiver down her spine. Thank heaven he hadn't called her 'sweet'! She would never have been able to explain that away if he had!

'Have you had time to consider my proposition?'

Put like that, in conjunction with the smooth intimacy of his deep warm voice, it sounded almost immoral, and she was very aware of the way Edmond was looking at her, then at Jackson, as if he'd been presented with a very knotty set of accounts.

'I'm afraid I haven't given it a thought,' she lied, matching the easiness of his tone. But her mind was screaming, *Go away! Just go away*! and she heard Edmond's light baritone enquire, just as casually, 'What proposition is that, dear?'

'You must be Edmond,' Jackson slid in silkily, the ice-green eyes not wavering from their scrutiny of the top of Susanna's downbent head.

Susanna, regarding the way her fingers were behaving, twisting and knotting themselves in her lap as if they had a manic life of their own, kept her face lowered in cowardly fashion, not daring to look at her tormentor. And he did torment her. Waking or sleeping, the thought of him, the very *idea* of him, tortured her brain.

'Time's running short, you know.' Only Susanna could detect the thread of a threat in his voice. 'But I'll give you a few more hours.'

To her utter relief, he left them then, going to lean on the bar, waiting to be served. Heads turned, eyes following him. He was a man people instinctively watched.

But before Susanna had time to finish her sigh of relief, Edmond wanted to know, 'Who the hell was that?' frowning irritably as one of the barmaids put their plates down on the table in front of them.

Susanna was grateful for the small interruption. It gave her a few seconds to pull her brains together, push away the mindless confusion Jackson Arne always managed to stir up in those normally orderly cells, and dredge up from somewhere a composed smile and a slight throwaway shrug. 'Some sort of sculptor, I gather.'

'Sculptor? Do we know of him?' Edmond spread his paper napkin across his lap, his pale fingers making it stretch as far as it would go. 'And what was the proposition he was on about? What did he mean by saying he'd give you a few more hours?'

With more speed than dignity, Susanna pushed a large wedge of quiche into her mouth. She didn't know how she was going to be able to swallow it because her stomach was churning, beyond control, and would probably violently reject anything she put into it. But Edmond would understand that one didn't speak with one's mouth full. Very full, in this instance. And it would give her time to consider exactly what she could tell him.

As much of the truth as she dared, she supposed, chewing grimly. As much as she could without hurting his feelings and revealing herself as the silly—and quite possibly wanton—creature she was. Or had been, she corrected herself hollowly. Never again would she allow Jackson Arne near her. That would be asking for trouble.

'I met him in the High Street one afternoon.' It wasn't a lie, it was merely leaving some of the truth out.

She fixed her eyes, which would keep straying towards the bar where Jackson stood, on the leaf of lettuce at the side of her slice of quiche. 'He asked me to pose for him, just for a few preliminary drawings for a commission he apparently has,' she added, pushing her mouth up into a tight smile, hoping she was sounding as though none of the edited information she was giving him held the slightest interest for her.

'Confounded nerve!' Edmond had finished his meal and laid his cutlery down tidily on his empty plate, dabbing his lips with his napkin. He ate quickly and neatly, and Susanna wondered if he would make love that way, then further horrified herself by envisioning the way Jackson would make love—wholeheartedly, savouring every moment, taking his time, extracting every last nuance of pleasure, making sure his woman did, too.

She must be turning into a sex maniac, she agonised, flooded with self-disgust, and Edmond grumbled, 'Aren't you going to finish your food? I hope you gave that uncouth bounder a piece of your mind. I can see the whole thing has upset you badly—you've gone very red—and I can't blame you at all! Take my advice and have a word with Sergeant Wainwright if he approaches you again. He's a sound chap—Wainwright, I mean—and will act discreetly with full regard to your position in this town. Respectable citizens should be able to feel that they can walk in their own town without being accosted by down-at-heel types with dubious propositions. Now do eat up, dear; we must be getting a move on.'

'I'm not hungry,' choked Susanna. How could Edmond understand that it wasn't Jackson's request that she pose for him that made her act like a demented schoolgirl in the painful throes of her first crush, blushing, unable to eat or sleep properly, twitching and trembling—it was the man himself! Edmond couldn't understand because she couldn't tell him. And she didn't even understand it herself. She turned to him impulsively. 'Edmond—can't you possibly arrange to take some time off next week? Couldn't you rearrange your appointments, pass some of your work load on to Fletcher? Please?'

All at once it seemed vitally important that they should get away from Much Barton, get to know each other. And it was useless to try to explain that although they thought they knew each other well enough to contemplate spending the rest of their lives together, she suddenly felt she didn't know him at all.

Oh, she knew what he looked like, what his likes and dislikes were, that he was a dutiful son to his widowed mother, was moderately ambitious, reasonable. But what went on inside his head? And how could he know her when all at once she knew she didn't know herself?

She tacked on, pleadingly, 'We could spend a few days at the coast, perhaps. Relax.'

'Really, Susanna——' he sighed, frowning at his watch. 'You know it's out of the question. I haven't been operating on my own for twelve months yet, and Fletcher's only been with me for six. It wouldn't be wise for me to take time off just now, and I certainly don't feel confident enough to leave young Fletcher on his own. We've discussed it all before, haven't we? Besides, you're going to decorate the spare bedroom for when Mother comes to stay with us after we're married. And we have our honeymoon to look forward to in January. Do come along, or we shall both be late.'

Curbing the sudden impulse to hurl the remains of her quiche at his head and tell him she wasn't, and never had been, particularly looking forward to their week's honeymoon in January, spent in Birmingham at his mother's home, Susanna jumped crossly to her feet, carefully not looking round to see if Jackson was still at the bar, and stumped outside in Edmond's wake.

Saturday was wet and chilly, which didn't please Susanna at all. She felt as though nothing would ever entirely please or satisfy her again.

Even her little home annoyed her. She had been so contented with it until now. And now the thought of the time when Edmond would give up his flat and move in here with her after they were married, the times when his mother would come on frequent and possibly protracted visits made her feel uncomfortably agitated.

Mallow Cottage was too small. That she hadn't felt it to be so, or viewed her future mother-in-law's proposed regular and lengthy visits with anything more than resignation before Jackson Arne's eruption into her life, was something her mind conveniently blanked out.

Her parents and Edmond were coming to dinner tonight. It had been arranged ten days ago. Susanna wished she had the strength of mind to pick up the phone and call it off. She didn't want to see any of them. She didn't know what she did want.

They were to have eaten outside on the patio, but the rain had put paid to that idea. The meal, eaten outside, would have been more relaxed. Never before had she realised that time spent with her parents, or with Edmond, come to that, was about as relaxed as piano wire.

She laid the table in the little sitting-room well in advance, taking care because of her mother's critical eyes, then wandered dispiritedly to the kitchen.

Susanna enjoyed cooking, but tonight she was keeping the menu simple. It wouldn't stretch her, although for some strange reason she felt she needed to be stretched to the limit, her mind completely occupied. But her father's ulcer was playing him up and her mother, very conscious of her figure and obviously determined to keep it slender and supple until her dying day, ate very lightly. And Edmond didn't care to eat anything rich in the evenings in case he got indigestion and couldn't sleep.

So they were having melon cocktail followed by sole in a light cream sauce. Which wouldn't do anyone any harm.

Upstairs, with two hours stretching drearily ahead

before her guests were due to arrive, she bathed and washed her hair and thought about Edmond and their future together. Not because she couldn't get him out of her mind, or because their future was such a delightful prospect that she couldn't resist taking an anticipatory peep, but because it stopped thoughts of Jackson intruding, as they did when her mind wasn't firmly fixed on something else. Preferably something disagreeable.

And was that how she regarded Edmond? As something disagreeable? No, of course it wasn't! While neither of them had ever pretended to deathless passion, they were fond of each other, had the same aims in life: successful careers, a comfortable life-style, two children, eventually. They respected each other.

Respected each other.

Perhaps that was the trouble, the root cause of her edginess. How could Edmond respect her when, after what had happened with Jackson, she couldn't respect herself? Oh lordy, was she ever confused!

Quite determined to get a grip of herself, to pull herself together, to salvage her sanity which, she felt, was rapidly deserting her, Susanna rummaged in her wardrobe for something to wear.

Tonight she would do her best to look as attractive as her face and figure would allow. She, who had never flirted in her life, or been flirted with, would flirt with Edmond—heavens, that would amaze him, wouldn't it? And she wouldn't talk about her work, because it bored her father, and she would do her best to keep up with Miranda's witty conversation because that would please her and perhaps show her that her daughter wasn't quite as dull as she thought she was.

Unfortunately, none of the garments she owned would ever make her look attractive, she decided gloomily. Everything was good quality, that went without saying because Miranda, who had such good taste, always insisted on helping Susanna when she bought clothes—something she only did when absolutely necessary. And all the clothes in the wardrobe seemed to have been designed to make the wearer blend into the woodwork, the colours dark and drab and supposedly slimming.

Snatching at her slipping determination to make herself look her best, and hoping for a minor miracle, she zipped herself into a dark green lightweight wool dress. The sacklike shape would cover a multitude of sins—that was the general idea, anyway—and the warm material would keep out the chill of the rainy evening, a chill which would settle permanently on her soul if she let it.

Her newly washed hair felt slippery and heavy, but she concentrated fiercely on trying to devise a more feminine and elegant style than the usual neat knot, and if the final result was on the odd side of interesting, she didn't allow it to dishearten her too much.

They ate dinner on the patio after all. By the time her guests had arrived the sun had, too, and Miranda, helping Susanna to unlay the table in the sitting-room, said, 'We'll be more comfortable outside. The evening's turned out beautifully, and this room's far too small for entertaining.'

'Well, you chose it,' grumbled Susanna with unprecedented tetchiness, out of patience with the performance of having to move everything, wipe the patio furniture dry and contend with feeling too hot in the dress that had been right for the chilly day it had been, but was far too heavy for the broiling evening it had become.

'What can you mean?' Miranda's eyes batted open in surprise, a handful of silverware clutched to her azure silk-covered bosom.

'When I was looking for a place of my own,' Susanna answered heavily, 'you and Edmond told me I needed something small——'

'And easy to run,' Miranda completed. 'But big enough for the two of you when you were married. That's right, we did say that, and this place is much more suitable than that rambly old Tudor farmhouse you had your eye on. Now, if you'll take the wine glasses, dear, I can manage the rest.'

So Susanna was handing coffee round, feeling the sun strike her back, perspiring steadily in the hot dress, her hair slithering down over one side of her flushed face. Far from flirting with Edmond, as had been her intention, and sparkling to impress Miranda who had once been heard to say that getting engaged would draw her clever but reserved daughter out of her shell and be a Good Thing, she had barely said two words. She had been irritated by Miranda's chatter, which she now saw as being too shallow for words, by Edmond's pomposity, by the way her father now seemed able to look at her without actually wincing.

For them, Susanna Bryce-Jones, an individual in her own right, just didn't exist. She was something her mother could manipulate and dominate, a suitable and sensible prospective wife and second right hand as far as Edmond was concerned, and a possible producer of a grandson to inherit, in the fullness of time, for her father.

For Susanna, who had channelled her life into her career, who had carelessly ignored or left other

aspects of her life in her mother's hands and,
latterly, Edmond's, it suddenly wasn't good enough.
And she surprised herself by actually experiencing
a surge of something that felt remarkably like joy
when she saw Jackson Arne leap over her garden
hedge.

No one else had noticed him yet, but Susanna,
sitting facing down the garden, found her mouth
curving in a slow smile as she saw him take a
couple of paces up the lawn, then slam to a halt,
his head thrown back as he became aware of the
family dinner party on the patio.

A totally uncharacteristic look of uncertainty
flickered over his face as if, just for once, he felt
unsure about intruding. And Susanna breathed out,
unaware until then that she'd been holding her
breath, as he continued on his way towards them.

She knew, with an inner certainty that astounded
her—considering the fraught circumstances—that
had he turned to retreat by the way he had come
she would have called out to him to stay, to join
them for coffee.

'Good evening, Mr Arne,' she said as he drew
nearer, finding it difficult to maintain her polite
hostess smile in face of the very definite grin that
was trying to break out. And she had to choke
back laughter when she saw heads turn, Miranda's
face a mask of icy fury, Edmond's showing outrage,
her father's evincing suspicion.

Because Jackson Arne, whatever else he was or
wasn't, wasn't a man anyone could ignore. Wearing
the most disreputable shorts she had ever seen—
old denim jeans unevenly hacked off to thigh level—
and nothing else at all, he looked magnificent. Pagan
male. His big, hard body gloriously tanned,
perfectly proportioned, his ruggedly attractive face

composed in spite of the laughter that danced in the depths of the slitted green eyes that held Susanna's.

From the corner of her eye she saw Edmond's face grow turkey-red, his cheeks bulging as, his courage bolstered by the presence of his future in-laws, he spluttered, 'Now look here, young man—' and Susanna cut him off smoothly, surprising herself.

'Won't you join us for coffee, Jackson?'

It was her coffee, her dinner party, her home. It was high time she began to assert herself in her personal life, and now seemed as good a time as any.

Jackson's eyes still held hers; he was taking as much notice of the others as if they'd been specks of dust on the ground, although he must have recognised her mother and her fiancé, thought Susanna amusedly. It took a real man to ignore the open hostility of the county's leading lady, her consort and her intended son-in-law.

'No coffee, thanks. I just dropped by to ask if you could lend me a pound of tea.'

Ice-green twinkled disarmingly into hazel, and laughter bubbled up inside Susanna at that absurdity. Ignoring Miranda's snorted, 'A *pound* of tea! *Really*!' she got to her feet.

'Come with me, I'll see what I can do,' she said, hearing her father's voice grumbling about something, knowing Jackson was following her.

Pleased at having taken the initiative for once in her life, totally disregarding what her parents and Edmond expected of her, she smiled up at Jackson as she closed the kitchen door firmly behind them, shutting them in, giving way to a surge of happiness

because the whole of today, until now, had been
so drab.

'I'm sorry about that.' His voice was low, husky,
his eyes troubled now. 'As you probably gathered,
I came to badger you into posing for me.' He
spread his strong sculptor's hands. 'I didn't realise
you were entertaining your nearest and dearest. I
want you to pose for me; I don't want to upset or
embarrass you.'

That's laying it on rather thick, Susanna thought
inelegantly, because he hadn't stopped to consider
a little thing like that when he'd returned her
dress!

Her heart turned over inside her, slowly and
sweetly, as she saw how genuinely concerned he
was, his vivid eyes troubled, and she wanted,
without knowing why, to hold him and assure him
that everything was all right, that she was neither
embarrassed nor upset. Strangely, she felt closer,
more attuned to him than to anyone else on earth.
Her smile widened as she told him, 'I'll find you
that tea.'

But as she turned to the wall cupboard where
she stored her dry goods, his hands stopped her.
'The tea was the only excuse for coming here that
I could think of on the spur of the moment.'

'A full pound of it, too!'

'I know. Insane, wasn't it?' He grinned wryly.
'You have that effect on me, sweet.'

He traced the outline of her cheek with slow
fingers, fingertips lingering briefly at the corner of
her mouth, trailing up to slide into her hair,
extracting the pins that hadn't already fallen out
over dinner so that it fell heavily to her shoulders,
a dark, silky waterfall framing her heart-shaped
face.

'You have lovely hair; you shouldn't scrape it back, sweet. And hasn't anyone ever told you that your body cries out for bright colours, light fabrics that move with you, that show off your fantastic figure, not swamp it? And don't hang your head,' he commanded gently as she tried to hide the flush of wondering excitement at his words. 'Every word is true, believe me. Look at me.'

Strong fingers lifted her chin, and tremors of something she couldn't name weakened her as she met his sensuous eyes.

'Believe me, sweet?'

Almost, she did. And she wanted to, so much. If the whole world thought her ugly, it didn't matter, so long as Jackson found her beautiful. And that acknowledgement had to be the strangest thing in the world, she conceded dazedly.

Their eyes held, and something tightened inside her, an invisible cord that was pulling her closer and closer to him, and she couldn't fight it, didn't think she wanted to fight it. Not right now.

He bent his head slowly, and although she knew he was going to kiss her she gasped as his lips touched a corner of her mouth. And slowly, still slowly, he created an exploratory, entirely sensual pressure, the tip of his tongue barely touching her softly parted lips.

The feeling that she was drowning, drowning, in a whirlpool of emotions she had never experienced before increased, swamping her, and she reached blindly for him, her fingers tangling in his hair, biting into the hardness of his skull. But he broke the kiss and held her gently away from him, his eyes lingering on her parted, trembling mouth.

'This isn't the time and this isn't the place. Remember your guests, sweet. You wouldn't want the upright Edmond to walk in on this sort of thing, would you?'

The dryness of his tone, the implication behind his words, jerked her back to the reality of what had been happening to her, and she shook her head, trying to clear it.

'I'll introduce you to them,' she told him throatily, 'and then you'd better go.'

She led the way out of the kitchen, her legs still unsteady, and the three at the table were looking through her to Jackson who was right behind. Their eyes were aggressive.

Whether it was then, or whether she'd unconsciously made up her mind much earlier, she could never decide. But she sounded very sure of herself when she announced, 'I'd like you all to meet Jackson Arne, near neighbour and sculptor. I have just agreed to model for him.'

CHAPTER FIVE

'You must have taken leave of your senses. Either that, or you've been pressured into it.' Edmond handed Susanna the trowel and stood up, the knees of his light tan trousers earth-stained. 'If he has put pressure on you, you've only to say and your father and I will deal with him.' Shooting her an exasperated look, he stamped the soil down round the newly planted lupin, breaking off its single straggly bloom.

Susanna stared at him blankly. She wasn't seeing him, or the litter of empty plant containers scattered on the lawn. Intent on her thoughts, she dismissed Edmond's words. *Pressured.* No, Jackson hadn't done that. When she'd made up her mind to pose for him, his threat to withhold information on what had really happened on the night she'd met him hadn't entered her mind. It was still a consideration, a vital one, but she hadn't given it a thought at the time.

'You haven't listened to a word I've been saying,' Edmond accused in the snappy tone he'd used with her since he'd picked her up to drive her over to the nursery to choose plants. 'Your parents, particularly your mother, were appalled.'

'I don't see why,' Susanna murmured. But she did know why. Miranda knew that for some reason, a reason she hadn't wanted to have explained to

81

her, Susanna's dress had spent the night at Jackson's home. The logical conclusion being that Susanna had, too.

'There's nothing reprehensible about posing for an artist. It's quite flattering. Besides,' she came up with the reason she'd been searching for and hadn't been able to find, even though she'd lain awake most of the night looking for it, 'I'm pleased to be able to help a struggling, unknown sculptor out. You never know, he might become famous one day, and the fact that I posed for one of his earlier pieces would give us something to boast about in our old age! Anyway,' she continued more seriously, 'he told me it's a big commission—probably his first ever, though I wouldn't know about that—and I guess it's important. It can't be easy to make a living carving stone, unless you happen to be a recognised big name.'

'You're too soft.' Edmond took his annoyance out on his trouser legs, slapping them furiously with his neat hands to get rid of the clinging grains of soil. 'I would never have thought it of you. You, of all people, to lay yourself open to ridicule by having anything at all to do with that uncouth, Bohemian, scruffy, no-good——' Words failed him and Susanna supplied, 'Layabout?'

'Precisely. At least you're not blind to that! When is the momentous,' his upper lip lifted derisively, 'first sitting to take place?'

'Tomorrow afternoon.'

'You are starting to decorate Mother's bedroom tomorrow,' he pointed out, his face red.

'I was. But now I'm not. Jackson dropped by this morning and suggested tomorrow and I agreed.'

'So our plans go by the board? I see!' Edmond began to stamp up the garden but turned, came back to her, and asked, his eyes narrowing suspiciously, 'Does he make a habit of dropping by? He seemed to know his way around—leaping over your hedge as if he had rights. How many times has he been here?'

'Are you jealous?' Susanna asked wonderingly, but there was scorn in his voice as he replied,

'Don't be so stupid. I can't see the day when I'd have to worry on that score. No, I just want to know how familiar you've allowed him to become. You have some quite nice things around you, and he's probably light-fingered.'

So he wasn't afraid of Jackson stealing her virtue, or her heart, or both, because he didn't think any man would fancy her. But he might fancy her silver cutlery, her few bits of antique porcelain! And that remark had to be a fair indication of his own feelings for her!

'He's been a couple of times, and he's no thief,' she retorted crossly, bending to pick up the scattered containers because Edmond just might see in her face the way she was remembering how each time Jackson had come he'd ended up kissing her.

Except for this morning. He'd been in a hurry, on his way to visit his father, and as soon as he'd made the arrangements for tomorrow he'd gone. But her tidy little kitchen had positively sparked with the electric tension of their growing involvement while he had been there, the warmth of his caressing voice, the unreadable message in his eyes, creating a tension that both exhilarated and terrified her.

'Well, I've said all I can. Quite frankly, Susanna, I'm disappointed in you. But if you're blind enough and stupid enough to get involved with that lout,

out of my hands. And I certainly don't want to quarrel with you over it. I shall just have to tell your mother that I've done my best to get you to see reason, and failed.'

So Miranda was behind this afternoon's sulky outburst, Susanna decided as Edmond walked away. She might have known. That Jackson Arne had proved himself as likely to kiss her as look at her, and that she would respond, would not have entered Edmond's head.

But her mother was no fool. She was a woman, and wouldn't have been blind to Jackson's powerful male sexuality. And she'd been there when he'd returned the dress, and she must be going frantic, wondering whether her daughter's indiscretions were about to be compounded—and ultimately discovered by the so-suitable Edmond Harding. He would never have approved of her posing for Jackson; he would never have given his blessing, but he wouldn't have made such a song and dance about it if he hadn't been egged on by her mother.

And Susanna wasn't blind, or stupid, as Edmond had implied. Jackson was struggling—she still had doubts about the legitimacy of his being in that hovel in the meadow—and he would grab at any opportunity, as she knew to her cost, of obtaining the free services of a suitable model for that all-important first commission.

And although he admittedly found her desirable, it was only a fleeting attraction, uninvolving. He would work his magic, flatter her outrageously, take his lovemaking as far as she would allow, until he had no further use for her. Then he would move on, forget her.

She knew all that. But the trouble was, he only had to walk into her line of vision to make her tremble for the delight she felt in his arms, the shattering excitement of his kisses. And it simply wasn't worth it, she acknowledged dully as she dumped the empty containers in the dustbin and went inside to make herself a much-needed pot of tea. Why should she jeopardise her safe, orderly future with Edmond for the sake of a few wild, sweet kisses from a light-hearted joker who had probably made love to more women than he could remember?

She and Edmond rubbed along well together. It was only since her meeting with Jackson Arne that she had become unsettled, annoying Edmond, hurting him, possibly. She had never been used to seeing a man look at her with desire in his eyes, flattering her, making her wonder if, after all these years of believing herself to be plain and unalluring, she had been wrong.

It had gone to her head, and surely she was sensible enough to understand that? There was no mileage in taking Jackson seriously.

Sipping her tea, she moved her left hand so that Edmond's diamonds winked coldly at her, and she told herself that although she had promised to pose for Jackson, and he was struggling and probably as poor as a church mouse, she would make it absolutely clear, as soon as she arrived at his place tomorrow afternoon, that he must never again lay a finger on her, much less kiss her, because if he did she would walk out.

In spite of her sensible lecture to herself, Susanna woke early to streaming sunlight, and the word 'sinful' popped into her mind and refused to pop out again.

Shivering as an unwarranted and entirely unher-

alded sting of excitement zipped through her, she
contemplated the day ahead. Would it be sinful?
That dratted word again! No, of course it wouldn't!

She could, if she wished, spend the morning
stripping the old paper off the spare bedroom
walls. But she didn't wish. How could she settle
down to anything so mundane when she would be
seeing Jackson again this afternoon?

Sinful was exactly the right word to describe
how she was feeling, she admonished herself
disgustedly as she flung out of bed, dragged on her
robe and went to make coffee.

The morning was glorious. Sipping coffee on her
patio, Susanna sniffed the air appreciatively. It was
fresh and pure, carrying the scents of her
neighbour's roses and the long meadow grass.

But, too wound up to relax and enjoy a lazy
hour or so, she washed her coffee cup and went
upstairs to dress. She needed fresh vegetables,
meat, so she might as well walk into town and pick
them up. She might also drop in to see Edmond,
suggest she make supper for him tonight, it would
be a way of healing the breach that seemed to be
opening up between them. The idea didn't enthuse
her, but she felt it was her duty to do something.

After buttoning up the bodice of her prim
shirtwaister, she automatically lifted her hands to
pin back her hair, then lowered them again slowly.
She would leave it as it was, loose, falling on to
her shoulders. She agreed with Jackson; it looked
better that way. It made her look younger, less
severe, more feminine.

Pushing away intruding speculative thoughts
about the coming afternoon, she walked briskly
into town, picked up her supplies and was on her

way back down the High Street when the window display in the small town's only boutique caught her eye.

Miranda didn't patronise the place; she said their stuff was flashy, but Susanna was no longer prepared to allow her mother's opinions to influence her.

Awkwardly at first, then with quickening excitement, she rummaged through the rails, tried on almost everything that came in her size, and staggered out again, clutching half a dozen bags. Her bank balance was considerably depleted but her heart was pounding with unaccustomed exhilaration.

She had chosen to keep one of her new outfits on, stuffing the staid dark shirtwaister into her shopping basket, under the cauliflower. She felt good in the softly pleated full cotton skirt, the swirly pattern in reds and greens on a paler green ground a new departure for her. The cotton top she had chosen to wear with it matched the darker green of the skirt and it hugged her, leaving her arms bare, dipping into a wide V at the neck, revealing the beginning of the mysterious cleft between her full breasts.

Feeling lighter and more feminine than she could ever remember, she mounted the stairs to Edmond's offices, her cheeks flushed and her hazel eyes sparkling with green lights that betokened a new knowledge—that of her potential as an attractive, even desirable, woman.

His secretary's double-take was reassuring, but Edmond's was not.

'Good lord! What have you done to yourself? You look like a gypsy.'

'Don't you like it?' The feminine, colourful

clothes had gone to Susanna's head like wine and she twirled around, her loose hair flying. Edmond mumbled, his neck going red,

'I don't know what's come over you just lately. Did you want to see me about something urgent? I'm expecting a client in five minutes.'

She should have felt deflated, but she didn't. Perching herself on the arm of the chair that faced his over the desk, she knew she could never marry him.

Perhaps she had known it for weeks. It had been there all along, at the back of her mind, smothered by the burden of other people's approval.

Everyone she knew, her parents in particular, had been amazed by her good fortune in finding a man who would want her—particularly a man as suitable as Edmond. And now the knowledge was out in the open reaches of her mind, clear to her. She could never marry him.

Their lives would run reasonably smoothly, side by side, if they married. Parallel lines, never touching, running through precisely-mapped country, never encountering real joy or sorrow.

Dull, utterly dull. And even if she never found the ecstasy of love, the passion or the splendour, she would be her own woman, free at last, not some creature pressed out of a mould made to her mother's and Edmond's specifications.

Emotional security no longer seemed enough, and she should never have allowed herself to be brainwashed into believing it could be, not if it meant drab safe years stretching ahead to dreary infinity.

A new woman with a clearer self-image had emerged from the dull chrysalis of conformity that had been built up from the viewpoint of others.

People who had never bothered to look inside her personal packaging to the true woman had made her what she had been, and she had helped, cementing the bricks together with her blind, unthinking acceptance.

But Jackson had found the cracks in the armour of her rigid conformity to the way others saw her; he had found his way to the waiting woman inside and had touched her with his magic.

That life wouldn't be a bed of sweet-smelling roses for the new self that was struggling to express itself, Susanna accepted. She was neither young enough nor foolish enough to imagine otherwise. If she refused to settle for second best, went looking for true self-fulfilment, then she would most probably get hurt, have to pick herself up from her knees many times and reach out for the stars again.

That she had no clear picture of what it was she sought, craved for, didn't trouble her right now. It was enough to know that her eyes had been opened wide enough to enable her to see before it was too late. The rest would follow.

'Edmond,' she said, as kindly as she could, 'I have to tell you that I can't marry you. I'm sorry, but it's all been a terrible mistake.'

Buttercups nodded on bent, slender necks, swaying, dropping small clouds of golden pollen as Susanna swung through the tall meadow grasses on sandalled feet.

She wondered if Jackson would notice that she was no longer wearing Edmond's ring. The scene that had followed her announcement hadn't been pleasant, and she knew she hadn't heard the last of it. But she put it out of her mind; the afternoon was too wonderful to spoil with thoughts of what her mother would have to say when she heard of the broken engagement.

A million birds seemed to be singing their hearts out from the sheltering woodland canopy, and the sun caressed her bare arms and throat, the long grasses and the soft fabric of her new skirt brushing seductively against her legs.

Vaguely, she felt that she ought to be feeling miserable, or guilty, or regretful and solemn about her broken engagement, but she knew she couldn't. She felt as if an enormous burden had been lifted from her shoulders. A different future lay ahead, enticing, uncertain, and she didn't know how she would cope with it alone, or even where the way ahead lay, but she was going to do her very best to enjoy it!

When the hovel came into view it didn't seem as hovel-like as she remembered. She had been painting a picture, using the palette provided by her upbringing, and now she was seeing it with newly opened eyes, choosing her own colours.

The squat stone walls and tumbled roofs were solid and enduring, offering a place of peace, a haven. It wasn't smart and it certainly wasn't twee. It was a simple statement in stone and timber and mortar.

And Jackson emerged from one of the doors, raising a hand to shield his eyes from the blinding sun. Again, he wore nothing but the hacked-off denim shorts, and her heart stilled, then raced on again because the picture he presented was a statement, too. One of pure, uncluttered male beauty. A golden god.

No double-takes for Jackson Arne. He accepted the new image without batting an eyelid, because after all, he had conjured it into being. There was a kind of magic in the man, she acknowledged humbly, knowing she was in the presence of something rare; her pleasure in him, in the golden afternoon, in her new clothes filled her until it spilled over in a wide smile which gave her classically moulded features a rare beauty.

All the same, she reminded herself as he walked towards her through the long grass, the sunlight glistening on bronzed skin, hard muscles, bright hair, all the same, she must not allow his magic to touch her too deeply.

She had been changing inside ever since she'd met him in the enchantment of moonlight, and although he didn't know it, he had shown her the woman who was inside the careful image that had been presented to the outside world for too many years. She would always be grateful to him for that. But the magic stopped there.

Jackson could hurt her, if she let him. She had a whole new future stretching ahead, and it wouldn't always be easy, and she most definitely wasn't going to court disaster by allowing him to weave his magic too closely about her, ensnaring her in a web that might be too strong to break.

He touched her hands once, just briefly, and their eyes held as the warmth in his met the warmth in hers and then he turned, walking with her in the direction of the cottage, and he said, 'Ready for work? Or would you like me to show you around first?'

'Whatever you like.' Susanna shrugged, smiling, not minding, because whatever he wanted was fine by her.

'We'll make a start right away,' he decided. 'I've been itching to begin drawing you for days.'

And that in itself was immensely flattering, and

she remembered the times when he'd said she was beautiful and how he'd told her to believe him. And she had, and it had altered her life, because the way she saw herself was the thing that mattered. And those thoughts reminded her.

'There is one thing, though.' Her feet stilled as he put a hand on her back, ushering her through the door he had emerged from earlier.

'What's that, sweet?' One dark eyebrow lifted and a corner of his firm mouth curled in the slow, enticing smile that had the power to make her heart kick.

Silly heart! she chided distractedly. He was a light-minded charmer who knew exactly how to get his own way. He wanted to make drawings of her, and until he'd done that he would continue—so effortlessly—to cajole and beguile. And then he would forget she had ever existed, because she'd be no more to him than lines on paper that were to be translated to stone. An idea in his head. And as long as she remembered that and accepted it, she'd be fine.

'Our bargain,' she answered him evenly, back in control again.

'Ah. Yes.' He pushed her firmly through the door, laughter enriching his voice. 'However, in your position—as a respected bank manager—you will understand all about the principles of bargaining from a position of strength. I will tell you what you want to know *after* I've made all the drawings I need.'

'But you said——' Susanna whipped round to face him, her eyes showing her hurt. She wanted to believe him to be a man of his word. Somehow it seemed very important. 'You told me you would tell me if I agreed to what you had to ask. You asked me to pose, and I've said I will.'

'Then I didn't phrase my ultimatum as precisely as I should have done.' Wide shoulders lifted in a wry shrug. 'Remiss of me.'

His hands came up to rest on her shoulders, holding her, the balls of his thumbs moving hypnotically over the hollows above her collarbone, sapping her strength, making her want to lean weakly against him, closer and closer, to feel the warm tanned skin against her cheek, to discover his exposed body with fingertips that were aching with the need of it.

'If I told you what you want to know now, there would be nothing to stop you walking out of that door. And then where would I be, with no bargaining power left?'

If only you knew! she groaned inwardly, twisting away from him because she couldn't cope with the heady sensations his nearness produced. One word, one caress from his eyes, was enough to persuade her into almost anything.

But that was something he must never know. And she had said she would pose for him. She had given her word. Did he think she was the sort of woman to go back on it?

'You don't trust me.' Her voice was flat and her eyes were cold.

This room, in contrast to the sitting-room she'd been in on the night of Lily's party, was bare. Austere. *He didn't trust her*. She counted items. A screen. A table laid out with the tools of his trade: drawing blocks, pencils, charcoal. A chair. A low dais. *He didn't trust her*. His very silence endorsed that. And his face was an expressionless mask as he walked into her line of vision again.

'Do you want me to?'

'That's a damn fool question!' she snapped back, stung. Everyone needed to be trusted by someone. Implicitly.

'Then I'll tell you.'

Her eyes flicked up to his, almost disbelievingly, and his own expression was puzzled, as if he were looking into his mind, not quite understanding what he saw there.

'There's no need.' Perversely, she turned away, her fingers wandering over the wooden back of the single chair. 'I take your point.'

'There's every need. I'll prove I trust you.' Jackson had made up his mind and he was back in bantering mood again as he told her, 'Nothing happened, sweet, I promise. I undressed you because I thought you'd be more comfortable that way. Then I tucked you up in bed. I took my dressing gown and left. No more.'

He closed in, standing behind her. The heat of his body, so close to hers, seared her. And something, a sweet vague hurting that clutched at her heart and swept up to catch in her throat, spread slowly to fill her, making her want to cry before it receded, leaving her shaken.

She had known, after the first panic had died down, that he wouldn't have done anything so demeaning as make love to a woman who wasn't capable of knowing what she was doing. He wasn't that type of man.

She had agonised over it, no use denying that, and the agony had been real, totally real when she had told him he wouldn't have made love to her because he wouldn't have wanted to.

And he had taken her in his arms and shown her the shattering reality of his wanting. She saw now that the initial agonising had merely been the smokescreen thrown up by her conscious mind because, subconsciously, she had known all along that he had his own brand of integrity, and it wouldn't allow him to do anything to degrade himself or any other living creature.

She hadn't wanted to admit that. She had wanted him to have made love to her. Still wanted it. And that was the most terrifying thing of all.

'Are you satisfied now?' Jackson moved closer, still behind her, and she was powerless to move as one strong sculptor's hand gently drew back the curtain of hair from one side of her face, then his head bent to hers, his lips tasting the exposed lobe of her ear, teasing the vulnerable hollow behind it. 'You can marry your Edmond, if you must, with a clear conscience,' he muttered drily.

That did it. It was all that had been needed to give her the strength of mind to move away.

'And that's another thing—you—you have to— stop—stop kissing me!'

To her disgust she sounded like a breathless juvenile, not the full-grown woman who had so recently become liberated from a demeaning self-image, implanted in the first place by people who hadn't had the wits or sensitivity to see that she was a person in her own rights.

And he must have heard the tremor of uncertainty, the trace of wistfulness, and he must have found it amusing, because the ice-green eyes lit with laughter as he tilted his head to one side, his long mouth curved upwards just slightly.

'And why not, since we both enjoy it so much? Ah——'His eyes sobered. 'How obtuse of me.' He plastered a look of sorrow on his rugged features. 'The lady is already spoken for, and the noble

Edmond would not be pleased by the idea of his
wife-to-be kissing another man. And enjoying it.
How foolish of you, sweet, to commit yourself to
someone. I don't believe in romantic commitments
of that kind—they tend to spoil so much that is
pleasurable in life. Or don't you agree? Tell me, is
Edmond as dull as he appears?'

He turned away, and his back was to her as his
fingers moved idly over the tools of his trade, laid
out on the table.

'Do you enjoy his kisses as much as you enjoy
mine? Does his touch fire your blood, make your
heart race like a wild thing? Or are you marrying
him because it's the safe and sensible thing to do?'

Susanna stared at the broad back, the muscles
clearly defined beneath the smooth tanned skin,
wide shoulders tapering to a slim waist, narrow
hips where the tight-fitting shorts were secured by
a leather belt. And she hated him then, hated the
hard look in his eyes as he swung round to face
her, the accusing look of rugged features that
suddenly seemed to be carved out of granite.

Jackson wasn't averse to taking his pleasures
where he could find them, lightly, without a
backward look because he didn't believe in
commitments. But he could frown his censure
because she had kissed him back, unable to hide
the responses of a body freshly awakened to an
unexpected sensuality.

That she had broken her engagement to Edmond
because he—with his teasing eyes and casual
kisses—had opened her eyes to the possibility that
life might hold more than dull security, was
something she wasn't prepared, now, to tell him.

'Perhaps,' she shrugged, pretending indifference.
'In any case, I want you to leave me alone.'

'Then it's hands off, is it? Okay. Fine!'

She had never seen him angry before. It gave a new dimension to his character, strengthening it because he held the emotion in check. And it puzzled her, too. She didn't understand why the simple request that in future he keep his hands off another man's woman should enrage him so. That she was no longer Edmond's fiancée was beside the point, because Jackson didn't know that.

His inexplicable reined-in anger stretched the tension. The tension had always been there; an awareness, a thin, almost-visible wire that pulled them together, surrounded them with its vibrancy. Now it was stronger, harder, and she could almost touch it. Trying to break it, she forced a light tone and asked, 'Is this where you work? Your studio?'

'I draw in here, put ideas down.' He dragged his breath in, making a visible effort to relax as he expelled the air slowly. 'The light's not good enough in here to carve by.'

His lips moved in a tight smile, but his eyes evaded hers. He was doing his best not to show the anger that still raged beneath the surface. He suggested woodenly, 'So we'll get down to work, shall we?'

Susanna nodded. Part of her was already regretting having told him to keep his distance. She hated the coolness her words had created; it made her feel lost and lonely, cold inside.

But it had been the sensible thing to do. His kisses could get to be habit-forming, leaving her with a craving for more and more.

It was best that he continued to believe that she was still engaged to Edmond. Best that he thought her hands-off directive had stemmed directly from a guilty conscience over her indiscretions of the

past few days. There was a measure of safety
there.

'Right.' He sounded brisk now, businesslike and
cool. And the jerk of his head was perfunctory as
he added, 'Use the screen over there. There's a
hanger—you can leave your clothes on that.'

CHAPTER SIX

'THE Roman goddess of beauty and love—a *Venus*—in big underwear!' Jackson roared. 'Have you gone mad! Good God, woman, I've *seen* your underwear! Can you just picture it? *Can* you? A life-size marble Venus in enormous——'

'Please——' Susanna's lips trembled and she sat down quickly on the single chair, her legs buckling. Jackson was breathing heavily, his nostrils flared, his feet planted wide apart as he glared down at her, his eyes transfixing her with their molten ferocity.

Then, as if the mists of rage cleared, his eyes became cooler, clear, focusing sharply on her quivering mouth, the unshed tears that swam in her peaty eyes. Snorting, he turned away, pacing the room, each movement taut, restless.

Susanna bowed her head, staring blindly at her knotted hands. It would be funny, if it weren't so terrifying. And it was terrifying; she knew, with inner dread, that she would end up, as always, doing exactly what he asked of her.

She had to do it; she had given her word, even though he hadn't explained exactly what would be required of her. He had already told her what she'd wanted to know, and a bargain was a bargain. But more than that, much more, was the utter conviction, shocking in its simplicity, that she would

always want to please him. She had to, if it were
within her power.

Such thoughts had battered at the inside of her
head in the moments of the first shocked realisation.
He wanted her to pose in the nude, and
the thought of it had made her feel ill with
embarrassment. Hence her tentative, pleading, silly
suggestion that she keep her underwear on—thus
provoking his furious outburst.

Turning, Jackson strode down the length of the
room, the muscles of his arms bunched as if he
were about to hit something. Wrenching a door
wide, he slammed through it, the sound of his fury
reverberating.

Alone, Susanna stared miserably at the blank
face of the closed door. It told her nothing. Only
her common sense, her logical reasoning power,
could tell her what to do now. The logical part of her
mind, the one that saw problems as mathematical
equations, solvable if one applied one's brain, told
her to go. Immediately. Sever the relationship, the
involvement. It was growing too strong.

She could always offer to pay for a professional
model. She could afford it, even if he couldn't,
and it would be a way of keeping her side of the
bargain.

But her heart, the inner core of her new-found
femininity, told her to stay, to be with him, help
him, do what she could.

Torn between the two, she was still there,
outwardly inert, when Jackson came back into the
room. He carried a large brown envelope and the
tension had left him—she could see that from the
look of compassion in his eyes, the gentle curve of
his mouth.

'Susanna——' He squatted down beside the chair

she sat on and his eyes, the hand that so lightly touched her arm, told her that he understood her reaction. 'There's nothing to be afraid of. I shouldn't have sprung it on you like that. You're not a professional model—but I was only thinking of what I wanted: you—and your perfect female body—for my Venus. It was selfish and thoughtless of me. Can you forgive me?'

She nodded mutely, spellbound by the hypnotic quality of his deep voice, the kindness in the ice-green eyes that seemed to look into her soul and read her confusion.

'Let me show you something. Explain.' Strong brown fingers extracted photographs from the envelope, holding them so that she could see.

They were all of a garden, different viewpoints of one part of a garden. Tall clipped yew hedges under a brilliant blue sky made a backdrop for smooth green sward, a sweeping amphitheatre for curving beds of tall white lilies.

'Here——' Jackson's fingertip tapped a spot in the centre of one of the photographs. 'Here a wealthy French bridegroom wishes to erect a piece of statuary—a celebration of love, of female perfection—in honour of his new and much-adored young wife. The Vicomte Hugo de Massin, no less, has commissioned me to do the work.'

Wicked green eyes slanted up at her and she longed to run her fingers through his tumbled honey-gold hair, cradle his face with her hands, and tell him not to worry about a model for the commission; she would do it. But her inbred sense of caution stopped her, that and his following, slightly contemptuous words, 'You would approve of him, sweet. Not only is he titled, he's immensely wealthy and has his business fingers in all sorts

of pies—vineyards, *haute couture*, international
banking—you name it.'

His voice had hardened, grown bitter, as if he
were envious of the man's wealth and power, and
her eyes misted over as pity for his obvious poverty,
his apparently rootless existence, clutched at her
heart.

She very much doubted if the Vicomte Hugo de
Massin, for all his breeding and wealth, could even
begin to match up to the physical perfection, the
sheer charisma, of the man who was Jackson Arne.
And he did have this commission, and presumably
it would pay well, so that was something positive.
She plastered a cheery look on her face, about to
tell him as much, but heartening words weren't
needed. She could see that his bitter mood had
vanished as he pushed himself up to his feet and
put the photographs back in the envelope.

'The subject and the setting demand a certain
formality of treatment. And the new Vicomtesse
doesn't go a bundle on abstracts, according to my
brief. So I'm left with the problem of realism
coupled with classicism, and I didn't have an idea
in my head that wasn't banal or derivative until I
met you. Come with me.'

She took the hand he held out to her, feeling the
supple fingers curve around her own, leading her,
she following blindly because this man had the
power to make her do just that.

'In you,' he told her, his voice holding a thread
of huskiness, an intimacy that bound them together,
'I saw that perfection of female beauty and love.
You are all woman. Magnificent. The essence of
female beauty, created for man's adoration—
majestic, yet pagan.'

He had led her from the room, his eyes

introspective now, already wrestling with his inner creation, not seeing her flushed embarrassment in hearing such words applied to her large and hitherto rather pitied self.

Outside, they rounded the house and came to the sheltered back of it, to a glass-roofed, open-sided workroom. A stout wooden bench ran the length of one side, covered with tools, and long fluorescent tubes hung overhead. Immediately, her eyes were drawn to a huge block of creamy-toned stone, and Jackson strode over to it, his eyes lighting as he ran long, sensitive fingers over the surface.

'This is where the essence of you will be, Susanna, for as long as the marble lasts. Feel it, feel how smooth, how cool and strong. Find, with your hands, the secrets it holds.'

Susanna laid her hands beneath his, her fingers feeling through the slight surface roughness of the marble to the smoothness beneath, smiling at the look of pride on his face as he told her, 'Serravezza, green from the quarry, chosen with care—believe me, with very great care.'

'How on earth did you get it here?' She hooked a slippery strand of hair behind one ear, tilting her head to look up at him. It was such an enormous piece of stone.

'On the back of a lorry.' His grin came suddenly, mocking her bewilderment, and he threw a casual arm around her shoulders and walked her back, round the outside of the building. 'Literally, sweet. The best marble is still quarried in Italy, and this piece was transported by lorry overland, across on a channel ferry and on up here. When our Venus is finished she will go back the same way. Would you like some tea?'

She nodded abstractedly, not thrown by his abrupt change of subject. The whole operation must have been horribly costly, but no doubt the French millionaire had footed the bill for the transportation of the stone. She knew it was none of her business, but she couldn't help asking,

'Will the Vicomte pay for her passage back?'

'It goes on the bill.'

They were in his kitchen now, a small dingy room, barely furnished, and Jackson had his back to her as he lit the Calor gas stove under the kettle, so she couldn't see his face, but his voice was curt, as if he had resented her question. But in spite of the repressive quality of his silence as he fished a teapot and mugs from one cupboard, a bottle of milk from another, she couldn't resist probing.

'And that outbuilding—where the marble is— that's your studio? Won't it be very cold and damp in the winter?'

'When winter comes I'll be long gone.'

The reply depressed her; she didn't know why, and her mood wasn't lightened when he ground out tersely, as if the words were pulled from him, as if he felt his personal life was his own and he wanted to keep it that way, sharing details of his life the last thing he wanted, 'This isn't my place, as I told you before. It belongs to a friend of mine who never comes here now, and when he knew I was looking for some place to work on the Venus he offered it to me provided I made my own arrangements regarding a temporary studio. Which I did. As you saw. And I'll use it, then leave it and move on. Satisfied?'

She would have to be, wouldn't she? Susanna thought glumly, accepting the mug of tea he pushed at her. There was a distressing edge of secretiveness in the ice-green eyes that met hers briefly, and there'd been a hardness in his voice when he'd answered the questions he probably believed to be impertinent.

And once again, tantalisingly out of the range of her groping memory, came the impression of something known. She mentally shook her head, taking her tea over to the tiny uncurtained window, staring out. She felt closer to Jackson each time they met; there had been an instantaneous rapport the first time she'd seen him and it was growing stronger all the time. There was no more to it than that.

And the tone of resentment, the touch of hardness—bitterness, almost—when he'd spoken of how she would approve of his wealthy patron, of the way he had acquired a temporary studio in order to be able to work at all, was natural enough.

And here she was, dithering, keeping him on tenterhooks. He couldn't afford to employ a professional model, and he seemed to think that she would suit, and he must be going through agonies wondering if she was about to refuse to sit for him, seeing his hopes of ever completing that important commission fly out of the door with her inhibitions . . .

She turned to reassure him at the exact moment he spoke her name, the word hanging heavily on the dim, silent air.

'Susanna——'

'It's all right, Jackson; I'll pose for you. I won't mind, really I won't.'

'Are you sure?' He closed the space between them, his eyes watchful, serious. 'You have to be quite sure.'

'I am.' Her voice was thick, difficult to get out, and he grinned suddenly, briefly, lightening the atmosphere.

'Good. Finish your tea and then we'll make a start. And don't be embarrassed. I'm totally professional when I work. I won't be seeing you, sweet, as a very desirable flesh and blood woman. I'll be seeing a dream in stone.'

He worked as though time had no meaning, stopping only to light lamps when encroaching twilight dimmed the room, his concentration intense.

After the first five minutes Susanna's acute embarrassment receded. Emerging tentatively from behind the screen, wearing nothing but the robe he had provided for her use, removing it with shaking fingers and taking the pose he required—the pose she had unknowingly auditioned for in this same cottage on the night she had first met him—had tested her courage to the limits.

But she had done it. For him. And not even the thought of what people would say if they ever got to hear how that ultra-respectable pillar of the establishment, the local bank manager, was posing—*in the nude, my dear, for a penniless stone carver*'—had the power to deflect her.

And the matter-of-fact way Jackson went about things, the complete lack of intimacy, helped. His attitude, as he made rapid drawings of the whole of her, or parts of her, took measurements, paced round her and drew again, relaxed her and she bore the increasing pain of holding the pose without a murmur. She wouldn't break his concentration by complaining.

And sometimes, when he remembered, he called

a break. She could hear him pacing round the outside of the cottage while she slipped her robe on and sat, resting. And sometimes, watching him as he worked, her body quickened with rising desire for him, hurting, and all the more painful because she knew that wanting this man was the most self-destructive thing she could do.

Her body seemed to grow softer as the hours went by, more fluid as she held the pose, becoming what he wanted her to be, and he, prowling now, now bending his bright head to make a detailed charcoal study of her right ankle and foot, was, in contrast, all hardness—muscle, sinew and bone. Not an ounce of spare flesh on his hard masculine frame, no softness—except in his eyes when he smiled.

At last Jackson emerged from the other place he had inhabited since he'd begun to work, drawing in a deep breath, shaking his head, running careless fingers through his hair.

'We've done it, sweet!' His grin was one of near rapture. 'One sitting! That's all it took. I knew you would inspire me!'

'You mean you won't want me again?'

A strange disappointment flattened her. It was just tiredness and reaction, she supposed as she flexed her stiff arms, rubbing them. They were aching with the strain of holding them up for so long. She couldn't actually *want* to have to go through all this again!

'No, you've done your bit—and perfectly, too! A few sculptors, and I'm one of them, prefer to work with only the aid of drawings, no working models. That particular technique does demand a heck of a lot of sustained effort and a clear perception of the final effect, but it works well for me.'

He didn't look in the least tired, Susanna thought grimly as she stepped down from the dais. Just elated, burning to get on to the next stage, which wouldn't include her. She felt empty. And his watchful eyes, mistaking her defeated look for exhaustion, softened as he held out her robe.

She took it from him, fingers fumbling as she tied it round her waist, their eyes holding, drawn as awareness leapt to sudden and shocking life, filling the space between them.

Sensing danger, she moved away; the man had replaced the professional artist, and she had to break the speaking eye contact, find something, anything, to say.

'May I see what you've done?'

'Of course.' His assenting words were stiff, as if her deliberate withdrawal had hurt, had pricked his male pride. But he flicked through his drawing blocks, finding the sketches he thought might interest her most.

Susanna looked at the bold, fluid lines that captured all viewpoints of the pose she had held, and she couldn't believe that she was looking at aspects of her own image.

'These are beautiful.'

Her voice was husky, awed, her throat constricted with tears because she was seeing perfection, an ideal, a very real talent, and it moved her unbearably.

'Surely you could sell your drawings?' she said at last, her practical mind surfacing with difficulty. She groped to find an idea, to hold on to it. She felt possessive towards him and she knew she shouldn't. She worried about him because he obviously didn't worry about himself, his future.

She wanted to find the way to a semblance of financial security for him. And practical things were easier to handle than the feelings that flooded through her, possessing her, as she held his work in her hands. And again the sexual tension was growing stronger, taking over as it did whenever they were together.

'If you sold your drawings it would be a way of earning some ready cash while you're working on your sculptures. For example, the gift shop in the High Street sells work by local artists, quite successfully, too. I've seen the sort of thing that sells and they have nothing like the quality of these drawings of yours,' she babbled on, her voice brisk now, and bright, only stopping when she saw the shuttered look in his eyes, blanking her out.

'I don't think so, but thanks for your concern.' He took the drawings from her hands, putting them on the table. 'But perhaps, when I've finished the Venus, you would like to have one or two of the drawings? As a remembrance?'

As a remembrance . The words had a funereal note. Susanna shuddered, cold, already relegated to the dead past. She tried to smile. 'Thank you, that would be nice, if you can spare one.'

His eyes, flicking to hers, were puzzled and she looked away, afraid that he might see too much.

'You're tired, sweet. And small wonder, it's——' He groaned and her eyes flew to his again. 'It's gone four in the morning!' He held out his wrist watch, inviting her surprise. 'You've every right to be exhausted.' Contrition darkened his eyes, pulled at his mouth, and she laughed shakily.

'You've worked all night.'

'*We've* worked all night. Come on,' he tapped her backside lightly, his eyes worried, 'get dressed. I'll take you home. You'll never be able to wake in time for work—I'm sorry.'

'I don't have to,' she reassured him. 'I'm on holiday for the next two weeks,' and could have laughed aloud, hugged him, for the almost comical look of relief that relaxed his expressive features.

'Right.' He expelled a deep breath, his eyes crinkling. 'As long as time doesn't matter to you either, I'll rephrase my instructions. Get dressed while I forage for something to eat and drink. Then I'll walk you home. I don't know about you, but I need to unwind before I can sleep after I've been working. Come through to the kitchen when you're ready.'

Time would never matter to him, Susanna mused as she dressed in the colourful skirt and cotton top. The spaces measured by the hands of a clock, the rigidly prescribed order in which more conventional souls did things, would mean nothing to a man who worked like one possessed when in the grip of the creative urge, slept when he could do no more and ate when he had to.

And she was looking forward to having supper with him—or should it be breakfast? Having a meal at gone four in the morning was a thing the old, precise, unimaginative Susanna would never have contemplated.

She was changing all the time. The process, once begun, seemed to be gathering momentum, embracing all her attitudes, making her admit there was a lot more to living than a safe career, a well-defined pattern which one stepped outside of at one's peril.

It might have been more sensible to decline to

stay, to go home, make herself some cocoa and fall into bed. But tonight was one of the last times she'd see him, so being sensible had nothing to do with it. He didn't need her to pose again, and already she sensed a change in him, too. The more serious, dedicated side of his character had been emerging ever since she'd arrived here, just after lunch. He would be totally involved in his work now, not needing her, and she would be forgotten. No need for him to waste precious time with her, not now he'd had what he'd wanted from her. So one final hour with him, relaxing, was something she owed herself.

He was not in the candlelit kitchen when she arrived, but he came in as she was standing there, disappointed because the room was empty.

'We'll eat in the sitting-room. You must be hungry.'

She was; she hadn't eaten since lunch, and then only a salad. She followed him to the cluttered sitting-room, and the general disarray didn't trouble her this time.

He had lighted the fire, the logs providing enough heat to keep the pre-dawn chill away, and the rickety table was set with chunks of granary bread, cheese, pâté, celery, a bowl of tomatoes and another of peaches and a bottle of wine. Which had to make it the strangest breakfast ever, she thought appreciatively.

They ate well, talking idly, both relaxing, and if they never met again, never had time to talk again, then this would have to be enough.

The fireglow, the food and wine, the soft ebb and flow of conversation, added to the piquancy of knowing that her time spent with this wickedly attractive, charismatic, entirely self-sufficient man was something Susanna would remember all her life, value, even though she knew he would soon forget her.

And then he spoiled it all. His words, not changing in their relaxed inflection, but all the more shattering because of that, forced her out of her contemplative mood.

'If you marry Edmond, you'll be throwing your life away. Can't you see that, sweet?'

She stiffened, tension suddenly aching in the back of her neck, tightening her jaws. Her head jerked up, meeting his lazy, mocking eyes.

'You don't love him,' he stated softly. 'If you did you wouldn't have come here with me, that first night. You wouldn't have enjoyed my kisses, my hands on your body, the way you did. So why not admit it and save yourself a lot of grief?'

He leaned forward in his chair, facing her across the hearth. Close, too close. If she stretched out her hand she could touch his. Touch the rugged face that the fireglow played over, softening the harshly modelled planes beneath the jutting Slavic cheekbones.

'I don't admit any such thing,' she defended, her head snapping round because she dare not meet his eyes.

'He hasn't taken you to bed yet.' His sureness took her breath away. 'If you were my woman you'd be in my bed now. Does he have ice in his veins? Because I know you haven't.'

She couldn't listen any longer. His sensual voice made her see things she didn't want to see. Shivering, she scrambled to her feet, facing him, her blood thudding thickly. 'You've got a nasty mind, mister! What happens between Edmond and me has nothing to do with you. So you kissed me.

So what!' Her breath caught, almost snatching her angry words away. 'You're an attractive man and, as you said, I don't have ice in my veins. And that's why I told you to keep your hands to yourself in future. I'm engaged to Edmond and I don't want to put myself in the position of cheating on him. And if it's any business of yours,' she flung at him, 'Edmond doesn't have ice in his veins, either!'

The implications of what she'd said were all lies, and she knew it, but she hoped he didn't. Because the lie of her continuing engagement was the only defence she had.

She twisted round, turning to the door, but Jackson was on his feet, stopping her, furious too, his fingers tightening round one arm, bruising, jerking her to him.

'You're hurting!' she spat, wrenching backwards, but his grip increased, punishing her.

'Not as much as you'll be hurting yourself if you go through with that marriage.' His eyes narrowed, a dull red stain covering his cheekbones, making the green of his eyes glitter. 'You'll be locking yourself in a prison with him. And you'll both be so afraid of doing anything that isn't wise and proper that you'll lose any initiative you ever had. You'll conform, you'll grow older and duller and you'll never know what love is. And if you don't know what love is I'll tell you what it isn't—it isn't a tidy emotion, one you can lock away in a filing cabinet if it gets troublesome.' His voice lowered, castigating her, and she hated him, hated the way he made her tremble inside, pulled her apart.

Then anger made her reckless and she hissed through her teeth, 'And what makes you think your method of dealing with love—or whatever you prefer to call it—is any better? Steering clear of romantic commitments, as you admit you do, is hardly less cowardly!' She brushed frantically at the hand that held her. 'I hate you, Jackson Arne— I really do!'

One final, desperate twist and she was free of his punitive grasp, heading for the door, running out into the meadow, ghostly in the dawn mist, her heart constricting painfully with an emotion she couldn't name, the taste of fear bitter on her tongue as she heard him following.

'Damn you, Susanna!' His arms reached for her, dragging her down, and there was raw violence in his voice. 'Damn you!'

Off balance, his weight brought her down. She fell across him on to the grass, gasping as his arms tightened, negating her tense struggles to get away from him.

He rolled over her, his hard thighs pinning her down as she thrashed her head wildly, her dark hair splayed on the dawn-grey grass, moaning her rejection of his violence as the ghostly mist rolled in, crowding them, touching.

'Be still!' His voice was tight with the violence she couldn't place in what she knew of him. And his hard body heated her, his fingers searing her with vivid sensation as he caught her chin, stilling the frantic twisting of her head.

Mist wreathed its silent way between them, dulling the glitter of his eyes, and as if to dispel the filmy barrier, he swore, low in his throat and savagely, before his head dropped and his mouth took hers in a bruising, crushing embrace that her fired anger met in her own need to punish, hurt.

But gradually the tenor of the kiss changed, without her knowing how or when. Lips were hungry, exploratory, but without the driving need to chastise. And another, deeper, sweeter need emerged, taking her over as she felt him groan her name, sparking an unfurling response that began deep inside her, spreading, covering her, inducing her frantic limbs to relax in seeping languor.

Slowly her hands moved across the tight skin of his bare back, getting to know the feel of his spine, ribcage, the shoulder blades that spread into the muscular strength of his shoulders, the strong column of his neck.

And his hands moved silkily, pushing beneath her top, his lips following until they found one hardened peak, and then the other, claiming her, and Susanna whispered his name, her body responding desperately, lost in the thick sweet pain of a desire she could no longer control or deny.

He was breathing deeply, roughly, and her hands reached up, her fingers twining in his hair, exploring the hard shape of his skull, pulling his head down to her softness, arching her body against his lower limbs which were hardened in intolerable need.

Nothing mattered but Jackson, his need for her and hers for him, the naturalness of this wild, sweet contact completing her. Without him she would never be whole.

The breeze shifted, sighing, winnowing through the tall grasses, and she breathed in the sweet scent of it, the clean male scent of him, and whispered his name just once.

Whether he loved her or not, whether he was even capable of loving anyone, was not at issue, not now. Only this contact mattered, completing them both, as natural as their bed of tender crushed grass and meadow flowers, their coverlet of opalescent mist.

Hungrily, he bent his head again to take her

parted lips. One hand held her head as he deepened the kiss, the other sliding beneath her skirt, his fingertips setting the heated satin of her skin on fire with feelings she had never before experienced.

Her body, following an instinct as old as time, moved beneath him, answering the rhythm of his, arching, inviting, and she heard his shaky, 'Oh God, Susanna . . .' then felt him stiffen, grow still.

And then he jerked away, rolling on to his knees, his head bent as though he were in pain. 'Jackson . . .' She moved on to her side, one hand reaching out to him instinctively through her confusion. 'Jackson—please——'

'Damn you, Susanna!' The words were torn from him, low, savage, thickened with pain. 'I want you like hell! But I don't poach on any man's reserves!' He jack-knifed to his feet, tension coiling through him. 'Get rid of Edmond, once and for all, before I take you as my woman!'

CHAPTER SEVEN

I LOVE him, Susanna anguished silently. Oh, how I love him!

Trailing disconsolately down the stairs after only three hours of fretful sleep, she stared blankly around her kitchen, not seeing anything, her mind churning.

Falling in love with Jackson Arne was a mistake of mind-blowing proportions, and she should have had the sense to prevent it happening. Drearily, she plugged in the electric kettle to make coffee.

Not even the new lemon yellow cat-suit she wore could raise her spirits. At least the old Susanna had been reasonably content, unaware that the world offered the kind of splendour that made the pulses quicken, the blood race, transporting the soul far above the realms of the familiar to a distant place where dreams came true and magic turned the most ordinary mortals to enchanted gods and goddesses. Maybe she would have been better off in the long run if she had stayed as she was, unaware and unawakened. She didn't know.

All she could think of was Jackson. Jackson. *Jackson*. The way that lock of hair fell over his forehead, the smiling ice-green eyes, the creative talent in his strong hands, the power his superb male body wielded over her senses.

She should have had more sense!

She had been aware, right at the beginning, of the irresistible pull that drew her to him like a moth to an unguarded flame or, more appropriately in her case, she admitted wryly, a half-crazed lemming following a call—only dimly heard but inexorably felt—hurling its silly self to destruction.

She sipped coffee moodily. Oh yes, she'd been aware of that fatal pull all right. And she'd tried to fight it in her feeble fashion, because she had known, deep down, that even if dreams did come true once in a while, and he fell in love with her, nothing but disaster could come of the relationship.

He was a footloose artist. He had come out of nowhere and would go back to nowhere, plaguing her, teaching her things about herself she might have been happier not knowing. A light-hearted charmer, a will-o'-the-wisp, flashing brilliantly for one moment in time, then leaving her in the darkness of his absence, going heaven only knew where in pursuit of his own inner dream.

There could be no place for a man like that in the life of the eminently sensible S. Bryce-Jones! So falling in love with him was a stupid waste and the problem had no validity, anyway, because Jackson wouldn't want a place in her life. Not a permanent one. He didn't make that kind of commitment.

Sighing, she rinsed her cup and dragged herself outside. She ought to water the new plants. They, like her spirit, were drooping. Life had to go on, as the saying went, even if her newly discovered feelings for him were pulling her apart.

Unwanted pictures of what had happened in the meadow at dawn writhed around in her mind. Out of anger, passion had been born, possessing them both with lusty new life, promising a release from the tension that had bedevilled them from the start. She had been driven wild with her need of him, mindlessly abandoning herself to his lovemaking.

And he had wanted her, there had been no mistaking the urgent reality of that. But he had withdrawn, leaving her aching, bereft, knowing that she loved him, had loved him since she had first seen him. And she remembered those words, those shaming words: *Get rid of Edmond, once and for all, before I take you as my woman.*

Before he had flung that at her she had been prepared, eager, to tell him of her love, to offer him the comfort of it to assuage whatever devil had been riding him at the moment of his unexpected withdrawal.

But his words had left hers dying on her lips, almost hating him but loving him, too. Take *her* as *his* woman! As if she were a tasty meal, all set out on a plate, a meal he would only condescend to consume when he was sure no one else had a prior claim! As if she herself had no say in the matter!

She had scrambled to her feet, pulling at her dishevelled clothing, almost sobbing in the confusion of loving and hating at the same time. Running blindly over the meadow, stumbling, not looking back, she had let herself into the house and hurled herself up the stairs and into bed.

Jackson wanted her on his terms—no mention of love or long-term commitments. And even if he had offered her his love—or even marriage— nothing could ever have come of it, because they could never fit into each other's worlds. So she had to make herself forget him. It wouldn't be easy.

'So there you are!'

Susanna groaned, hunching her shoulders defens-

ively as she listened to the clack-clack of her
mother's high heels crossing the patio. She carefully
put down the watering can, her depression
compounded, and met Miranda's snapping blue
eyes with blankness.

'I've been trying to get hold of you since
yesterday afternoon. You weren't answering the
phone, so I drove over last night and let myself in
and sat and waited. I waited until well after
midnight. So where were you?'

'Out.'

'I know you were out, dear.' Miranda bared her
teeth. 'Don't be so tiresome. And do let's go
inside—unless you want all your neighbours to
know your business.'

Resignedly, Susanna followed her mother's trim
figure. She could have done without this visitation,
couldn't she just!

Miranda put herself on one of the chintz-covered
armchairs, perched on the edge, far from relaxed,
looking very county in her sage green linen skirt,
oyster silk shirt and single strand of pearls.

'Well, where were you? You must have known I
would want to contact you as soon as I heard what
poor dear Edmond had to tell me.'

Susanna sighed. It came from the soles of her
feet and dragged its way right through her. The
next half-hour or so promised to be most unpleasant.
It would be a long time before she heard the last
of the way she'd broken her engagement.

'I was posing for Jackson Arne.'

'Until well after midnight?'

'Until four in the morning.'

'Until——!'

Miranda was speechless, but her expression of
outraged horror said it all. And when her features

assumed a carefully bland mask, Susanna knew the big guns were being made ready for action.

Her movements a masterpiece of controlled elegance, Miranda extracted a cigarette from her enamelled case, lit it and slid the case back into her handbag. Blowing a plume of thin blue smoke, her slight smile not touching her narrowed eyes, she remarked slowly, 'I see. He is an attractive devil, that macho hippie of yours, I'll give you that. I had my suspicions about your relationship from the word go. And that sort of thing is all very well if you can be discreet about it, dear, but you're so gullible, and I don't suppose he knows the meaning of the word discretion. That type never does; they don't play the game to our rules. All brawn and no brain and only one thing on his mind—to put it delicately. And I only hope your little romps with him didn't have anything to do with the way you stupidly broke off with poor Edmond.'

Susanna's face ran with hot colour. She was old enough to conduct her life in any way she thought fit, without having to account to her mother! And the way Miranda had been speaking, making her relationship with Jackson sound so sordid, was beyond bearing!

'I love him!' she growled. She hadn't meant to tell a living soul, but it had simply shot out, just like that, in defence of them both. 'There's nothing disgraceful about that—and he's very talented——'

'I'm sure he is, dear,' Miranda put in smoothly. 'In certain directions. But, to put it crudely, that sort of thing never lasts long beyond the honeymoon. Especially after the bills start to roll in. And in your case, dear, you'd be the one who would be paying the bills while he slouches around, playing at being some kind of artist, wearing next to nothing—if his garb on Saturday evening was anything to go by—looking sexy for some other little nitwit while you go out to work to keep him.' She stubbed her cigarette out, smiling thinly. 'I take it he wants to marry you? Hence your idiotic behaviour with Edmond?'

'My breaking with Edmond has nothing to do with Jackson.' Susanna felt like screaming, but that wouldn't solve anything, not in the long term, and she wasn't sure if her statement was true.

'No? I'm afraid I don't believe you.' Miranda gave her daughter a long, assessing look. 'You've lost your head over that layabout. I don't want to hurt your feelings, dear, but I'm afraid this has to be said. Just stop to think for a moment—use that excellent brain of yours. Ask yourself why an enormously attractive man like that would give you so much as a second glance. He must be able to have his pick of nubile little things, so why should he bother with you—you're not exactly film star material, are you, dear?' She crossed her long, silk-clad legs, leaning back, more relaxed now. 'If you stop to think, you'll realise that your Mr Muscles has done his homework and discovered that you have a well-paid job, a nice little home, and parents who are likely to leave you a great deal of money—not to mention property. Need I say more?'

'You've said enough.'

Susanna's face was white, her fingers knotted on her lap. All through her life her mother had gently but thoroughly put her down. She could see that now, and in spite of her determination to be her own woman from now on, and not see herself through the eyes of others, it hurt.

'Just for once you've got it all wrong,' she said crossly. 'Jackson's never mentioned marriage, so you're way off mark. And if anyone had his eye on the main chance, it was Edmond. You introduced us—son of an old friend of yours, you said. Cosy little dinner parties, Sunday lunch, family picnics. You threw us together, and all the time you were dropping hints. Big ones about how successful I was in my career, how sensible, careful with money. Showing him all over the family house, driving him round Dad's land, making it clear that one day it would all come to me. Oh, you weren't as crass as I make it sound. You can be subtle when you want to be. But it was there all the time—what a catch I'd be for a man who could bear to have a big plain woman as his wife.'

'I don't like your tone. And at least Edmond is suitable.' Miranda got to her feet, collecting her handbag, her mouth compressed to a tight line. 'I'll go, since you're in no mood to be reasonable. But I'll leave you with two things to mull over. The first being that Edmond has given his word that he won't hold anything against you, Susanna. *Anything*—and that's a big concession and probably more than you deserve—if you come to your senses and take back his ring.' She swept to the door, pausing. 'The second is this—I shall find your Mr Arne and tell him that if he marries you, your father and I will leave everything to your cousin Eric. Then we can all sit back and see how fast your Mr Muscles can run.'

Susanna was stunned by the degrading and horrible picture that threat brought to her mind, unable to speak as Miranda sailed out. Her mother always had the last word. But not this time! She caught up with her outside, getting into her car.

'Save yourself the trouble,' she advised, breathing hard. 'I told you how I feel about Jackson—which was very foolish of me—but he's not interested. He's already told me he's not the marrying kind.'

The day stretched emptily ahead. Her mother's threat held no real terror for her now. Miranda was no fool; she could weigh things up. She wouldn't want to embarrass herself by confronting Jackson now that she knew he wasn't interested in her daughter's prospects.

Each day was empty, right through her holiday. Susanna redecorated the small spare bedroom—not that Edmond's mother would be using it, of course, but she had already bought the materials and might as well use them. She worked in the garden, and fought the temptation to walk across the meadow and find out how Jackson was getting on with his Venus, and make her peace with him—if there could ever be anything approaching peace between them, which she doubted.

But he hadn't tried to contact her, so that meant he had put her out of his mind, was probably engrossed in his work, never giving her a thought. And why should he? He had wanted her, but it had been a passing thing, soon forgotten, sublimated quite effortlessly in the challenge of his work. And if someone were to mention her name to him he'd probably say 'Who's she?'.

She had to stop thinking about him. She had to.

The last few days of her holiday had been cloudy, and on the Saturday morning the heavens opened. Deciding she would get just as drenched in the time it would take her to walk to Barnham's farmyard to fetch her car as if she walked the whole way into town, Susanna buttoned herself into her old grey gaberdine, tied a plastic rain-hood over her hair and set out, her old brogues squelching through the puddles.

She wouldn't have bothered to go at all, but she was running out of food supplies; when she rounded the corner of the High Street she wished she'd stayed at home and starved. Because Jackson was there, only a few yards ahead along the pavement, all six foot three of him, impressive in a rain-wet black leather jacket, dark denim jeans.

He wasn't looking her way, and she was glad of that, because he was holding a protective arm around the sassiest little blonde Susanna had ever seen. She was tiny and slender, dressed in a scarlet raincoat, her dainty feet supported by high-heeled scarlet ankle boots, her long curling blonde hair kept dry by the frivolous scarlet umbrella Jackson was carefully holding over her.

And as if all that weren't bad enough, the face that was laughingly tilted up to Jackson's warm smile was pretty and delicate and vividly unforgettable.

A knife-thrust of searing jealousy jabbed and twisted inside Susanna, propelling her jerkily through the swing doors of the supermarket. Staring blindly at the shelves of cat food, she tried to get a grip on herself.

Jackson Arne, in common with most males, preferred his women to come in tiny packages—pretty and blonde and appealing. And S. Bryce-Jones was big and sturdy, just right to model for a massive stone carving and that was all. The mental jab of seeing him with the blonde was just what was needed to bring her to her senses, wasn't it?

A feeling of hugeness, a dragging sensation of heavy clumsiness, fell over her as she miserably trudged back to collect a trolley. Then she pushed it morosely up the aisle, unable to remember what she needed to buy.

Rainwater was dripping off the hems of her gaberdine into her brogues, and it was trickling in spiteful rivulets off her plastic hood, down her neck, dropping off the end of her nose.

Grumpily, she grabbed a jar of coffee and dropped it into her trolley with a rattly clump, and a warm lazy voice spoke in her ear. 'Get out of the wrong side of bed this morning, sweet?'

Susanna's face flooded with hot colour and her stomach did a few somersaults and began to tie itself in knots. Not looking round, she cannoned off, pushing her trolley through the Saturday morning shoppers. She couldn't bear to look at him, or at the scarlet-clad, little and lovely lady who would no doubt be clinging prettily to the big man's arms. She couldn't stand the inevitable comparisons, the possible introductions. She didn't want to know!

'Hey—what's the hurry?'

Her arm was taken in a grip that almost dragged her off her feet and her trolley swung round, colliding with his, blocking the aisle. Jackson's voice had been raised and he was holding her, laughing down at her with his wicked green eyes, his rain-darkened hair plastered to his skull in intriguing flattened curls. And everyone was looking in their direction with avid interest.

'I am sorry,' apologised Susanna to a woman she recognised as being one of the bank's customers, disengaging her trolley from Jackson's, clearing the obstruction. Her heart was pattering wildly. At least the little blonde was nowhere in sight. To Jackson she said coolly, as if she'd only just seen him, and wasn't overjoyed about it, 'Good morning. Horrible weather, isn't it.'

'Shall I make the right banal response, sweet?' A shaggy eyebrow lifted, a smile curling his mouth at the corners. 'Or shall I ask you how you've been, tell you I've missed you?'

'Neither is called for.' Tight lips moved just enough for the words to be audible as she lifted a packet of something, willy-nilly, from the nearest shelf. She did wish he'd keep his voice down. *Everyone* was staring at them!

'Then come and tell me what to buy——' He gestured widely. 'These places confuse me. Tell you what,' an arm gathered her to the breadth of his chest, making her heart thump with his proximity, the elusive scent of wet leather, cleanly virile male flesh, the warmth of his breath as he bent his head closer. 'You choose what we'll have for our suppers all next week. Come over in the evenings and cook for us both while I work—I don't make the time to bother for myself. And after we've eaten we can take up where we left off. Have you given Edmond his marching orders yet?'

'No.'

'No to what? No you haven't finished with Edmond? Or no you won't cook my suppers?'

'No to every damn thing!'

The words came out on a groan and her limbs weakened, heat flooding through her at the memory of exactly where they had left off, in the meadow at dawn almost two weeks ago.

He was still pursuing her, hounding her outrageously, and this time he wasn't wanting a model, he was wanting her. And for the sake of her sanity, she had to fight him.

Her face, under the unbecoming plastic hood, ran with fiery colour, and no matter how hard she tried to extricate herself from his bear hug, she wasn't making any progress. Making an utter fool of herself, she wailed inwardly—tussling with this extrovert, very determined giant in full view of at least two dozen people who recognised her!

'Let me go!' she muttered, low and angry. 'If you don't mind making a fool of yourself in front of the half of Much Barton who will promptly go and tell the other half what they've seen, then I do!'

'You *are* afraid of the image slipping, aren't you?' His voice had a growly note she didn't like, but he did release her. 'Afraid to let anyone see that the awesome bank manager lady is as human as anyone else?'

'Get lost!'

'Manners, Miss Bryce-Jones! Manners!' His sudden grin was infuriating. 'And I've no intention of doing any such thing.' He was right behind her as she steered her trolley down the aisle, his voice rough velvet. 'We've unfinished business, you and I. And no one gets rid of me until I'm ready to go.'

He had abandoned his own trolley and he stuck with her, commenting aggravatingly on every item she selected, reading from the labels in his carrying voice, putting things firmly back on the shelves if he thought the ingredients, or additives, might be bad for her health.

Susanna was mortified, and tried to pretend he wasn't with her, but that was impossible, even she could see that. And Tom Griffiths, the store manager, was peering over his till, his face crumpled with displeasure, and she offered him a wavery smile which didn't seem to mollify him.

'Shut up!' she hissed at the unconcerned Jackson out of the side of her mouth. 'Do you want to get us both thrown out!'

Jackson's good-natured shrug told her he didn't mind one way or the other, and he was with her at the checkout point, lifting the basket she'd packed with careless, hurried fingers, right at her side as she pushed out of the doors to the street.

The rain was still sluicing down, and he didn't seem to mind. His eyes, his voice, held the hypnotic quality she found so hard to resist and her annoyance evaporated meekly when he suggested, 'Let's dive in somewhere for coffee. I want to talk to you.'

The idea was tempting, but she knew she ought to give him a frosty brush-off and plod her wet way home; she couldn't understand the feeble 'Okay, then' that left her lips, or the pleasure that pulsed through her, warming her.

And the rain didn't seem to touch her now, either, she thought bemusedly as they walked the length of the street. She was cocooned in the circle of her love for him, strangely, almost against her will, and certainly against her better judgment. She should be running, but her love for him was all that mattered at this moment, her love and the strong vibrations that emanated from him, reaching out and covering her, making everything else recede.

She should be fighting it, not weakly letting herself flow with it. But even when a gust of wind snatched the plastic hood from her head and Jackson said, 'Let the horrendous thing go,' she hadn't any more sense than to watch it bowl down

the street and smile back up into his eyes. She was
a fool where this man was concerned, and she
didn't seem able to do a thing about it.

They didn't go into the Feathers Hotel, which
was very up-market and was where Susanna and
Miranda always went when they met for coffee.
The steamy side-street café Jackson took her to,
with its plastic tables and loud piped music, was
more in his range, she supposed. He wouldn't be
able to afford the prices charged at the Feathers.

But it was warm and cheerful in here, and that
was what she must try to be. It didn't pay to
antagonise him; she had learned that much. Better
to portray cheerful friendliness—tempered with a
touch of indifference—as if she could take his
company, or leave it, it didn't matter to her. It was
safer that way.

So when he brought their coffee over and asked,
'Would you like a cake with that?' she was able to
achieve a light smile and the sort of throwaway
comment she'd make to any friend who'd asked
the same question.

'Don't tempt me. I can't afford to get any fatter.'

'Any fatter?' His eyes darkened, caressing her as
he took the chair opposite. 'You're not fat, sweet—
you're Junoesque, magnificent. I can't stand scrawny
women.'

'Really.' Blood throbbed in Susanna's temples as
she bit back the retort 'I suppose you don't call the
tiny blonde in red scrawny, then'—she wouldn't
give him the satisfaction!

He was very laid-back, very cool, that darned
smile playing along his beautiful male mouth, his
strong hands loosely cradling his coffee cup. And
the sound system was pushing out music, filling the
steamy air, surrounding them, Jennifer Rush singing

'I am your lady', and Susanna wanted to cry with the pain of it.

She could be his lady, for a little time, while he still wanted her. All she need do was tell him she'd broken with Edmond, offer to cook those suppers, and let him take it from there.

But she couldn't do it. Already she knew she would never find another man to match up to him. To give herself to him, and lose him, would be sentencing herself to a lifetime of aching loneliness, of regrets and the pain of unfulfilled wanting . . .

Getting to grips with herself, she swallowed around the lump in her throat and sought a relatively safe topic. 'How's the Venus coming along? No problems, I hope?'

'Not one.' His eyes challenged her. 'Come over and see for yourself?'

'I'd like to.' She sipped coffee carefully, and when she put the cup down her smile was calmly polite. 'I might walk over tomorrow, if I've time.'

She had all the time in the world, but she wouldn't be going. She might be a fool, but she wasn't quite insane yet. But she had made the conventially polite response for nothing, because he told her, 'I won't be there tomorrow. I'm riding over this afternoon to pay my father a duty visit. I won't be back until some time on Monday morning.'

Her relief was tempered with disappointment, though why she should have felt either, she couldn't imagine. Surely her fool brain hadn't been toying with the idea of actually walking over, after all? She picked him up, showing a polite interest.

'Where does your father live?'

'Just the other side of Shrewsbury.'

'But that's over thirty miles—did you say you'd be riding there?'

'That's right. Another coffee?'

'No—no, thanks,' she dismissed the offer with an agitated flap of her hand. 'Ride what? Not a bicycle, surely?'

'Motorbike. It's handy to get around on,' the cleft at the side of his mouth deepened, 'and cheap to run.'

'But the weather!' Susanna hated to think of the drenching he'd get. He probably didn't even have proper waterproof clothing. He just didn't look after himself properly; he'd already said he didn't make time to cook for himself! And that worried her. 'If you like,' she offered in a rush, unable to stop herself even though she knew that any further involvement with him was emotional suicide, 'I could drive you over. I wouldn't stay, just say hello to your father perhaps, and leave you there. I've nothing much on, only I'd have to pick you up again on Sunday evening because I'm back at work on Monday morning.'

'No, thanks.'

His eyes were cold, a slatey green that told her nothing, except that he considered her offer impertinent, or worse. She had been so sure that he'd jump at the opportunity of travelling in comfort.

'Shall we go, if you've finished?'

He was distancing himself, and she could take a hint, although she couldn't understand his sudden change of mood. She ought to be thankful that she'd been saved from the consequences of her rash offer. His curt refusal meant she wouldn't have to see him again—except, perhaps, by chance.

But misery dragged at her spirits as she plodded at his side through the wet streets. She had tried to take her shopping basket from him, but he'd brushed her aside, saying he was walking her way in any case and that no woman carried a heavy load while he was around to do it.

'How gallant!' she'd snapped, stupidly hurt by his withdrawal, but he hadn't responded and they'd walked in silence, the only sounds the pattering of the rain and the splash of their feet on the wet pavements.

She didn't invite him into the house, but he pushed his way in behind her just the same, dumping the basket down on the kitchen table, watching her from unreadable eyes.

'You're not wearing his ring,' he remarked levelly, and Susanna's fingers, unbuttoning her drenched gaberdine, stilled, clenching as wary tension snaked through her.

Jackson moved forward, watching her intently, and he was speaking to her with his eyes now, his withdrawn mood gone. Capitulation to the command expressed in every line of that hard male body, expressive face and eloquent eyes was near, very near. The tension tightening, drawing her to him.

Hastily, babbling because she had to put up some kind of barrier, putting the lie between them like an unscaleable wall, she fabricated wildly, 'Not at the moment, no. It—it was too tight. I've had to take it to be altered, that's all.'

'That's all, is it?' His lips compressed to a savage line, the inexplicable rage, the violence, surfacing hotly again as his hand shot out to fasten round hers, wrenching her forwards so that she tumbled against him, her head falling against the breadth of his leather-covered chest.

Jerking back, she spat out, 'Let me go! What the hell do you think you're doing?'

'Teaching you a lesson, sweet!' he ground out as

his mouth descended on hers, demanding a response she knew she shouldn't allow herself the luxury of giving.

His hands were on either side of her head, his fingers splayed in her wet hair, the tips pressed hard against her skull as his tongue invaded the parted sweetness of her lips with seductive ease. His body pressed urgently against hers, sending wildly clamouring messages her own body was no longer capable of refusing. Instructions from her feverishly active brain weren't getting through, and it blanked off feebly, leaving her body in control.

She didn't know how her wet coat got to be lying on the floor, but it was, and Jackson's hands were moving over her heated body, moulding it, exciting it beyond endurance, beyond caring for the consequences that might reach far into the future. She didn't care what might happen. She wanted his lovemaking. The floodtide of her desire was relentless, urgently demanding a release from the hot, aching need that spiralled through her, a release that only he could bring.

Warm fingers of one strongly supple hand deftly unbuttoned her blouse, his lips following, feathering over the exposed skin, his hand pulling aside the white cotton of her bra, and Susanna was lost, drowning in sensations only he could invoke.

'You want me as much as I want you.' His voice was thick, deep, as he teased one hardened nipple, the warmth of his breath on her skin, the intimacy, shaking her. 'What are you afraid of?' His head came up, his eyes locking with hers as his hands continued to work their magic on her flesh. 'Tell me why you're set on marrying a man you don't love, rather than coming to me, where you belong.

Tell me why, when I only have to touch you to make you want me.'

Abruptly, his hands fell to his sides and he stepped back. She might have fallen, but pride held her upright, scrabbling at her disordered clothing, her face ashen.

'Nothing to say?' He turned away, walking to the door. 'Then I'll say it for you. You're afraid to give. You've spent years believing you've nothing to give, and now I've shown you that you have, you're afraid of that, too.' He faced her briefly, burning eyes raking her. 'Wake up, sweet, before it's too late. You'll be my woman yet, believe me. I want you, and I always get what I want. I don't give up, ever.'

CHAPTER EIGHT

SUSANNA had just finished signing the letters for that afternoon's post when Graham, her chief clerk, pushed his head round her office door. It was Friday afternoon again; the weather had resumed its heatwave status and Graham looked like she felt—as if he couldn't wait for the weekend either.

'There's a Jackson Arne to see you, if you can spare him ten minutes.' The clerk's face was blank, bored with life, the wry lift of his shoulders saying it all. 'He doesn't have an account with us, but——'

Her features were equally impassive, but her heart was jumping, her breathing quickened. She hadn't seen Jackson since last Saturday morning, but he'd been right inside her head all the time, his parting words reverberating in her skull like a tolling bell, the nerve-racking expectancy of the possibility of his seeking her out at any time, anywhere, keeping her on a knife edge of suspense.

And now he was asking to see her. She could say she was busy, but that would only be postponing the inevitable. She matched the clerk's shrug, knowing he was waiting for her reply. 'You may as well show him in, Graham.'

And when he came he filled the room with his presence, negating everything else so that the two of them might have been the only inhabitants of a distant world. His potency, the assured male virility

136

of him, was an almost tangible thing, shocking in the neat, neutral space she habitually occupied. And his mocking eyes stripped her, cutting through the veneer of her grey cotton twill suit to the warm reality of the woman beneath.

Her eyes veiled under heavy, lowered lashes, Susanna watched covertly as he looked around before settling his long frame in the precisely placed chair facing hers across the desk. He was something else, a free pagan spirit in this conventional room, conceding nothing, assured of who and what he was. The frayed, dust-filmed jeans mocked the status quo, as did the tight black T-shirt that defined the power and grace of his superb upper body.

Betraying pulses throbbed at her temples and in her throat, and she hoped he wouldn't recognise how deeply he disturbed her. The silence was stretching, tightening, filled with unspoken thoughts, memories, images of lips that had clung, bodies that had asked questions, received answers . . .

Jackson looked absurdly relaxed, she noted enviously, as every nerve end in her body seemed to jump simultaneously when the character line at one side of his mouth indented, producing the slight lopsided smile that dragged the breath out of her body. The laughter lines around his eyes deepened, concentrating the green of his eyes to sparkling emerald as he told her, 'I want you to invest in my future. As a banker you'll be prepared to take a calculated risk?'

'Could you be more precise, Mr Arne?' Her voice was impersonal, surprising her, clipped but not dismissive—yet. She hadn't known she possessed such acting ability, because she was sick inside, hating the knowledge that everything—his flattery, his lovemaking, the outrageous way he'd pushed himself into her life and turned it upside down, had been leading up to this. A direct request for a bank loan.

The light had gone out of the day, and the eyes that met his across the neat, polished desk were dark and defeated. Something inside her had died.

'Do you have an account at one of our other branches?' she made herself ask, the tight line of her mouth emphasising her hold on authority, formality.

'I don't.' Green eyes teased, rising above the aura of supremacy she was trying to conquer him with. 'But I offer collateral—my hands, my eyes, my imagination, my body, the man I am.'

'I'm afraid not.' Her formality was increasing, deliberately so. Only by distancing herself, only by seeing him as a penniless supplicant, a man with no steady occupation and no fixed abode as far as she could tell, and not as the man she had so crazily come to love, could she prevent herself from crying aloud in her disappointment in him.

It cut her like a knife and made her feel she was bleeding inside from the hurt of knowing—no matter how unlikely the opposite had been—that nothing good could ever come of their relationship. Always, madly, there had been at the back of her mind a faintly flickering hope, and now even that, poor feeble thing that it had been, was dead.

'Banks don't work like that,' she said heavily, not looking at him. Glancing pointedly at her watch, but definitely not looking at him. 'We look for something more tangible than an idea in someone's mind when we loan money.'

'You don't think I'm a good risk?' Humour

edged his voice and Susanna shook her head mutely. She couldn't speak.

She stood up awkwardly, terminating the interview. Every muscle in her body seemed to have lost the power of co-ordination, and her breath fluttered raggedly as he got to his feet, too. This had to be the end. The ending of a strange and rather wonderful thing that had tilted her world on its secure axis, opening up new vistas for her and meaning nothing at all to him.

'Susanna——' Jackson was closing the space between them, not leaving as she had expected, and her mouth went dry, her face a blank wall, only her eyes showing her hurt, and these she kept deliberately lowered, concentrating on the pattern of the brown and fawn carpet. If he was going to try to charm her into making him a loan then she would need all the control she was capable of to stop herself from throwing up.

He came close, but he didn't use his hands to touch her, his eyes did that, compelling hers to lift with unspoken, undeniable command.

'I don't want the bank's money.' Green eyes held hers, their unmistakable message sending flickers of longing through her, uncurling wantonly in her loins, weakening her. 'I want you. You know that. And I'm asking you to throw your bonnet over the windmill, to invest your future in mine. I want you and I mean to have you, so do yourself a favour and think it over. We're wasting a hell of a lot of precious time.'

'You say you want me—do you mean permanently?' Her heart jolted, her teeth catching at her lower lip to stop herself confessing her love for him, because even if he admitted he loved her, as she loved him, nothing good could ever come of it. Their lives ran on different levels. Like oil and water, there could be no cohesion.

'Nothing in this life is permanent, sweet.' He did touch her then, his hands as soft as his voice as they rested on her shoulders, sending messages all along her nervous system. 'Impermanence is the sad condition of the human race. Don't ask me to answer for the future, because I can't. You've built your life on neat calculations, tidy equations. You cling to your rock of common sense and long-term security, but what you can't see is that the rock is lying on shifting sand, because nothing lasts, nothing is predictable. All we can do—all I'm asking you to do—is to recognise the truth of what there is between us. I want you to come to me, go where I go. I'm never long in one place, sweet. My work takes me all over. I'd want you with me. It would mean giving up all this.' A sweep of his hand dismissed her office, her desk, her symbols of status. 'Follow your heart for once, sweet, instead of your head.'

Blocking her mind to the hypnotic quality of that deep voice, she twisted away. She dared not listen to what he was saying, *dared* not! Staring out of the tall sash window, seeing nothing, she bit out, 'You're asking me to throw away everything I've worked for to go with you? Where? Wherever the mood of the moment takes you, I suppose?' Her shoulders bunched, the tight band of tension constricting her chest, painful and deadly, angling through her body to catch at her throat, aching . . . aching . . . 'You'd expect me to live as you do, like a gypsy, to stay with you as long as you fancy me? The answer's no, Mr Arne. Even if you went down on your knees and begged it would still be no.'

'I don't beg,' he told her tightly. 'Ever.'

He moved to stand behind her, so close that the heat of his body burned through her clothing, her skin, reaching to the very core of her being. And his voice held deadly purpose. 'I don't beg, but I always get what I want. And I'm willing to wait, if I have to, until you're ready to trust me, ready to trust what I know your heart tells you.'

She didn't hear him leave, but the emptiness of his absence closed over her like the cold breath of the tomb, and she closed her eyes and allowed the release of tears because he was offering her, for a space of time, the moon and the stars, and she was far too sensible to reach out and take them.

An hour later she exchanged a few words with the security guard who was starting to lock up, and stepped out on to the pavement.

The High Street was baking in the sun, and the few shoppers moving aimlessly, complaining about the heat as last week they had grumbled about the rain. Feeling reasonably confident that she was looking outwardly composed, she stopped to buy fruit and eggs, talking quite normally when spoken to, although inside her mind was on another plane.

What Jackson suggested was impossible. A nebulous offer, a fantasy, the only reality their mutual desire. For him the affair would last only as long as his wanting continued—two weeks, two months, two years—if she were very lucky and someone like the ravishing little blonde didn't claim his attention much sooner. But for her it would be a forever thing. She loved him. And it was all impossible.

Her body must have taken over, like an automatic pilot, because she didn't realise she was at home, doing her usual routine things, until she scalded her hand slightly as she was pouring boiling water into the teapot.

Biting back a sharp expletive, she held her hand under the cold tap and knew she had to sort herself out, once and for all. Jackson wanted her, and she had to resist because the few weeks or months he offered were not enough. But in the state she was in, if he continued to pressure her—and it was obvious that he meant to do just that—then heaven only knew what would happen. She couldn't trust herself.

So when Edmond walked in through the open kitchen door she was almost pleased to see him. Jackson wouldn't push things too far while he believed she was still engaged to someone else. She had had painful and humiliating evidence of that!

'I've brought back the things you left at Lily's.' Edmond put the plastic carrier he was holding down on the floor. 'I'd have returned them sooner, but I wanted to give you time to think things over. I would like to talk to you, Susanna.'

'Have some tea?' Almost, she wished she hadn't broken their engagement, that she could find his company as comfortably pleasant as she once had done. Edmond represented sanity and safety. He would never pull her apart, stir her emotions until she didn't know whether she was on her head or her heels. But she had tasted the heady magic of champagne, and plain tap water could never satisfy her again.

'Not for me, thanks.' He pulled out a kitchen chair and sat at the table, tweaking his trousers, careful of the razor-sharp creases. 'But you go ahead.' He watched as she poured out her own cup of tea, her hands unsteady. 'I haven't told anyone yet, apart from Miranda, about our broken engagement—not even my mother.'

'She'll have to know.' Susanna sat down heavily; she didn't want a post-mortem, but if Edmond was insisting then she supposed she owed him that much.

'I hoped you'd come to your senses.'

'Maybe I did.' She sighed, drained, finding the effort of concentrating, of talking to him, almost too much. 'I came to my senses when I realised it wouldn't have worked. We don't love each other. It wouldn't have been fair to either of us.'

'We respect each other and we have many things in common,' he objected tetchily. 'We both knew that was enough to base a sound marriage on.' An uncomfortable red stained his face. 'Until you got involved with that shiftless so-called sculptor.' He cleared his throat, slanting her a sly look. 'Miranda and I have talked the whole thing over. And I'm perfectly prepared to forget it ever happened, never mention it again.'

'Mention what, exactly?' Susanna snapped, appalled by what she was hearing.

'That you got the hots for that layabout, of course.' Edmond's face grew redder as he shifted in his chair, avoiding her eyes, and she snapped,

'That's a disgusting thing to say!'

'It's only the truth.' He looked at her then, his eyes beginning to bulge, and she couldn't even feel sorry for him now. He made her feel ill. 'I don't pretend to understand it, I would have thought you had more self-respect. But Miranda suggested that you'd been knocked senseless. Having that macho type hang around you had gone to your head because that sort of thing had never happened to you before. Miranda thinks you'll soon get over the novelty and regret throwing me over. So I'm telling you I'm willing to forget and forgive.'

He shuffled to his feet, his agitation making his movements unusually clumsy and awkward as he made a grab for her across the table, holding on to her as he sidled round it and dragged her into his arms, his breathing heavy, his eyes hot.

'If you've developed a taste for caveman tactics, I think you'll find I can accommodate you.'

He was holding her in a rib-crushing bear hug, and it shocked her to immobility because physical contact between them in the past had been kept to a chaste minimum. But now his mouth clamped on hers, their teeth clashing as he used the strength of his jaws to force her lips apart, and Susanna felt nothing but a sickness in her stomach.

Beating her fists against him, trying to push him away, only increased his determination, but he did release her squashed and hurting mouth for long enough to grunt, 'I know how to have a bit of fun, too, you see!'

'I shall throw up in a minute,' Susanna took the opportunity to snarl, pushing at him frantically. 'Is this another of Miranda's little suggestions?'

'What's that got to do with it, if it's what you like?'

'You've got to be joking!' She was breathing hard now, angry green lights sparking from dark hazel eyes, and he silenced her protests with his mouth, his horrible fat tongue making her gag. And she knew she had to stop him before she was sick.

Her hands shot up to his head, reaching for his ears. If she pulled them really hard, twisted, too, he would have to let her go because it would hurt and he was a baby when it came to any kind of pain. But her fingers stayed in his hair, shocked to stillness by the deep, cutting drawl,

'Am I interrupting something?'

Jackson! Her face, which had been pale with revulsion, flooded with bright hot colour as Edmond lifted his mouth, releasing hers, and her dazed eyes took in Jackson's sardonic stare, the downtwist of rage on his lips as he stood at the open door, watching them.

'Nothing that can't be continued.' Edmond stepped back, straightening his tie, a smirk on his face. 'I'll see you tomorrow, Susanna. And we'll take the precaution of locking the doors.'

Open-mouthed, her heart pattering like a trapped animal, Susanna watched as Edmond sidled past Jackson and out of the door. Jackson couldn't fail to put the wrong interpretation on what he'd just seen and what he'd heard from Edmond.

And that could only be to her advantage, she told herself shakily. It would reinforce the impression that she was going to marry Edmond, no matter what Jackson did to try to come between them.

The silence thickened. The tension in it made her want to scream, and his eyes were damning her. He moved from his position in the doorway, just two paces into the room, and the tension increased painfully. Susanna shuddered as the shock waves of the unspoken emotional violence filled the space between them. Fighting desperately to hold on to herself, to stop herself from throwing herself into his arms and blurting out everything—her love for him, her broken engagement—she met his accusing eyes.

What right had he to look at her that way, as if she had betrayed him? Whipping herself up into a semblance of anger, she continued her mental dialogue with herself: so he'd walked in, uninvited, and found her in the arms of the man he still believed to be her fiancé. So what was wrong with that?

He answered for her, his eyes hard, his upper lip lifting in derision as he told her, 'That stuffed shirt will never make you happy.'

'So what's that—to you?'

'We've been through all that, and I don't intend repeating myself yet again.'

Even though his attitude seemed relaxed, his long legs slightly straddled, his thumbs hooked into the pockets of his jeans, the aura of menace came over strongly, and Susanna fought back, verbally placing her defences. Her love for him was a real and hurting thing, and she wanted to hurt him in return, to make him suffer as she was suffering, because there was nothing else. Could be nothing else.

'You make me tired,' she rasped out bitterly, taking her teacup to the sink and tipping the untasted contents away, busying herself because something inside was driving her to hurt him but she couldn't bear to see the pain in his eyes when she did. 'You breeze into my life, decide you fancy me, kiss me a couple of times—and think that gives you the right to turn me inside out!'

She twisted the hot tap on, rinsing her cup, and the gushing water added a background of ferocious sound to her words, spurring her on. 'You say, in your arrogant know-it-all way, that Edmond wouldn't make me happy. How can you possibly know that? And don't bother to tell me.

I don't want to know what you think. But I'll tell you something, just for a change——' She didn't turn to look at him, just concentrated on the cup in her hands, the hot water gushing wastefully from the tap. 'You couldn't do any better. What do you have to offer?' She forced a sneer to underline her words. 'A few weeks—or months, if I hold your interest that long—living in a borrowed shack. Moving on to where? A tent under a hedge? And you think that would make me happy? Maybe I prefer what Edmond offers.'

'That's what we have to find out.' Amazingly, Jackson's voice was warm, almost amused, and he came to stand beside her, turning off the tap. 'You'll wash the pattern off that cup.' He took it from her, placing it upside down on the drainer. 'Stop knocking your head against a wall, sweet. Let me dry your hands.'

He took a towel from the rail near the sink and patted her hands dry as though she were a child, and Susanna couldn't trust herself to look at him. She reached for the chair Edmond had used and sank down on it, her knees shaking.

She was buckling all over, reaction setting in. He had so many moods, most of them inexplicable, and he used each and every one of them to confuse her, defeat her.

Taking the chair on the opposite side of the small table, he reached for her hands, holding them as if they were impossibly fragile and might break beneath his touch.

'Susanna, look at me.'

She couldn't. She couldn't meet those eloquent eyes and still retain her grip on the small vestige of sanity she had left.

'What's the point?' The words were dragged

out of her slowly, denying everything she was trying so hard to smother. 'You've made yourself clear. You want me, but I'm engaged to Edmond. He happens to be the better risk. End of story.'

'It needn't be.' Lean brown fingers tightened fractionally and her pulses fluttered uncertainly, responding to his slightest touch with the abandonment she knew she had to suppress.

'But it is. It has to be.' If he could read the anguish in her voice it was just too bad. She was still fighting, but she couldn't control all her emotions. They were too many and too strong. And it didn't help to feel the sheer masculinity of him clear across the table, feel its messages rising through the contact of their touching hands, suffusing her entire being. She gulped, her voice thick with pain, 'You ask me to leave everything, to go with you. I know nothing about you and it doesn't make sense, any of it.' She tried to pull her hands away, but Jackson tightened his grip. He would never give up.

'It makes sense to me, sweet. The moment I saw you, I wanted you, and not just as a model, either. And don't tell me the feeling wasn't mutual, because it was. It still is. But Edmond's between us and you're using him like a damned shield!'

His voice had hardened, grown colder, and Susanna met his eyes at last, her own accusing now. 'That's good old-fashioned lust. You'll get over it. And I don't intend to be around to get thrown out when you do. And as I don't intend saying any more about it, you'd better go.'

She made a more determined effort to free herself from the hands that held hers captive, but he pulled her arms across the table and held her hands against his chest.

'Feel my heart, Susanna,' he ground out. 'It's real. I'm real. What I feel for you is real.'

His narrowed eyes compelled her, holding her unwilling gaze, drowning her. And without her brain having any part in the matter, her fingers uncurled against the smoothness of his T-shirt, touching the warmth of him. The steady beat of his heart transmitted its rhythm to her own, and tentatively her treacherous fingers began their own mindless exploration of the hard, well-defined pectoral muscles, the concavity above his collarbone, the powerful shoulder muscles, the warm, tanned skin of his throat.

Her heart thudded wildly and her eyelids grew heavy as her gaze left his and dropped lingeringly to the sensual curve of his strongly moulded mouth, the lips slightly parted, softened, as his fingers began their own investigation of her captive arms. Sliding upwards and beneath the short wide sleeves of the blouse she wore, finding the intimate hollow beneath her arms, feathering out and down, just slightly, to the smooth skin of the rounded, swelling sides of her breasts.

Susanna's breath caught in her throat, her longing for him too much to bear. But she had to bear it, to fight it . . . Hastily, she dropped her hands from his shoulders, letting them lie on the table, but that was a bad mistake, because her ill-considered action had trapped his hands, pressing them closer to her body, and now the long fingers moved more purposefully, splaying over her aroused breasts, cupping them, feeling their weight, teasing . . .

She sprang to her feet, her face running with

hot colour, her rapid movement upsetting the chair, and she turned her back on him, breathing heavily, willing the snaking, burning desire he'd aroused to leave her.

'You're crazy—we both are,' she told him, her voice husky with the need he had woken in her. 'I want you to go away, leave me in peace. You're asking the impossible. Go to you, you say——' She walked over to the sink, leaning against it, her eyes closed, the pain around her heart making her breathless. 'You don't say for how long, or where we'd live, or how we'd manage if I gave up my job. I know nothing about you; you've made sure of that. There've been times when I've mentioned your father, or how you earn a living, when I've seen you clam up right in front of me. You came out of nowhere, and as far as I know you're going nowhere.' She turned then, slowly, forcing herself to meet unreadable eyes. 'But you'll be going there without me.'

'Why?'

His question was simple, but she couldn't find an answer. If he couldn't understand what she'd been trying to say, then too bad.

He got to his feet, spreading his hands, palms facing her. 'Where I came from isn't important, or it shouldn't be. And the only way you'll find out where I'm going is if you come with me.' He advanced, closing the gap, and Susanna's throat tightened as she swung away, staring out of the window at the lengthening shadows on the smooth green grass of her lawn. 'You see me as a peasant, a wandering hobo—way below your elevated class. Well, you'll just have to accept me on trust, believe that I'd never willingly hurt you, do anything to make your life less happy.'

He was closer, his voice lowered. Calm. Slowly, he moved in, standing right behind her, his arms around her, his hands spread flat against her stomach.

Susanna gulped, swallowing tears, fighting the raging desire to turn in his arms. He'd got it all wrong, but she wasn't about to put him right because he didn't miss a trick. She didn't care what class he came from; his parents could have been a couple of tramps, he could have been born in a ditch, for all she cared. She didn't cling to outdated class values, the way Miranda did.

Jackson lowered his head, his bright hair mingling with the smooth darkness of hers.

'Accept me for the man I am, Susanna. Marry me.'

She stiffened at his words, her whole body rigid. It was what she had heard in her dreams at night; it was what she was afraid to even think about in broad daylight. And it weakened her already shaky defences. But he didn't allow her time to gather her wits, find something to say.

'Don't answer now. Think it over. I won't bring any more pressure to bear; I promise that. It's entirely up to you now. And when you've decided, come and tell me and I'll abide by any decision you make. You know where to find me.' His lips brushed her neck tenderly, just below her ear, and she shuddered convulsively, wanting him, needing him, loving him. But not daring to admit to any of those things.

'And when you've given Edmond his marching orders and promised to marry me, we'll visit my father and give him the good news.'

He moved away and she didn't turn to see him go, but she knew his parting words would stay in her memory for ever.

'Think very carefully, sweet. Trust me, join with me in every sense of the word. Trust me with your future, your happiness—because if you can't do that we have nothing.'

CHAPTER NINE

SUSANNA spent a sleepless night, and when she crawled out of bed at dawn she was no nearer to solving the problems that had kept her awake, tossing and turning all through the long lonely hours of darkness.

Dragging her robe on, she ran her fingers irritably through her tumbled hair and stumped downstairs to the kitchen. It was dim there, but she didn't bother to switch on the light. The grey dawn haziness suited her mood.

She made coffee, drinking it standing up. Jackson's proposal of marriage had shocked her, shattering her preconception that his type of man didn't go in for that type of relationship. He had admitted as much, once. So what had changed his mind? He had talked of wanting, never of loving. Did he see marriage as the only way of getting her into his bed without the conscience-prickling spectre of Edmond hanging over his head? Did he want her *that* much?

It seemed a heavy price to pay, but perhaps he viewed marriage as something that could be easily jettisoned once its useful purpose had been served?

She didn't know. She simply didn't *know*!

Setting the empty cup back on its saucer with a violence which should have shattered it but didn't, she unlocked the back door and went outside into the cool morning air, not even the glory of the dawn chorus registering on her fractured mind.

His reasons for offering marriage were an enigma, but her reasons for refusing him—as she would do by her complete silence on the subject—were not. He was a virtual stranger. What did she know of him? Nothing. He was insecure, as hard to pin down as a will-o'-the wisp, unplaceable in her recognition. A bad risk. It would be the height of insanity to give up everything she had ever worked towards—a good job, a home of her own, her right place in the scheme of known and safe things—and trust him, as he'd said she must.

Her inner agonising brought a scowl to her face as she prowled the length and breadth of her small garden. She had to use up some of her restless energy somehow. And what on earth would Miranda have to say if she did 'throw her bonnet over the windmill' and marry Jackson? It didn't bear thinking about!

Her restless feet brought her to the low hedge at the end of her garden, facing the meadow beyond. Fingers of sunlight were now touching the heads of the trees which were up to their necks in mist on the far side of the meadow, beckoning . . . She only had to cross the expanse of dew-damp grass to find him . . .

Shying away from that thought, she calmed her mind by telling herself that she only had to sit tight, wait it out. He had said he would be long gone by the time winter came. Two, three months at the most, and the cottage in the meadow would be silent, cold, unoccupied. Jackson would be gone and she would never see him again.

Tears coursed silently down her cheeks, and she didn't know she was crying until a sob broke in her throat. Hesitantly, her fingers touched her wet cheeks and then her face was in her hands as she sobbed for what she was losing, throwing away.

At last, when the sun finally broke through the mist, touching her, warming her, she turned her back on the meadow and walked slowly into the house.

The vision of the empty cottage, of a winter meadow backed by skeletal trees, stayed with her, haunting her right through the weekend, up until the Wednesday morning. And at eleven that morning she carefully put down the folders she'd been sifting through then, as though sleepwalking, left her office, left the building, unaware of the raised eyebrows she left behind.

Not knowing where she was going, not really interested, she walked for miles, the exercise calming her mind until it was sufficiently quiet to accept the inevitable without raising its usual noisy objections.

She loved Jackson, and always would. Whatever happened, wherever their futures lay, she would be with him. To spend her life without him was unthinkable, and she didn't know why it had taken her so long to figure it out. Nothing mattered but her love for him. If the day ever dawned when she knew for a certainty that she couldn't reach out to him, go to him, then that day would be the first day of a life she would spend carrying around a dead heart. The mind-pictures of the empty cottage, the winter meadow, had opened her mind at last to that undeniable fact.

Once the decision had been made, accepted, she retraced her steps, her swinging stride buoyant

with happiness. She loved him; only that mattered.
A future without him was no future at all.

She re-entered the bank, bestowing beaming
smiles all round, then went to her office to type
out her resignation, signing it with an unaccustomed
flourish. There was no way she could hold down a
full-time responsible job after she and Jackson
were married. He was a wanderer, going where the
mood of the moment took him. Marriage wouldn't
change or tame him, she knew that. She also knew
she didn't care; she would a hundred times rather
have an insecure future with him than any amount
of security and material comfort without him. It
was what he had meant when he'd asked her to
accept him for what he was, trust her happiness to
him.

Well, she had and she did, and never before had
she felt so gloriously happy. She had capitulated at
last, followed her heart instead of her head, and it
felt wonderful!

That evening Susanna faced herself in the bathroom
mirror and tried to rationalise her disappointment.
Winged feet had sent her flying over the meadow
to find Jackson, but he hadn't been there. The
house was locked and the block of marble, which
he had obviously been working on, was covered
with a sheet of plastic, his tools lying where he had
left them. There'd been a note attached to the
cottage door with a drawing pin: 'If you drop by,
sweet, I'll be back Thursday lunchtime.' Somehow,
in those heavily scrawled few words, there had
seemed to be a plea, and her heart had almost
disintegrated with love for him.

And perhaps it was best that he'd been out,
because she looked a mess. She looked about a

hundred years old, knocking two hundred. Four sleepless nights in a row had left her looking dead, her eyes dull and purple-shadowed, the lines of her face dragged down with weariness.

Tonight she would sleep and tomorrow, as soon as the bank closed, she would go to him—looking her best!

Besides, she had reluctantly agreed to meet Miranda and Lily Anstruther for lunch tomorrow at the Feathers. She didn't want to go, but when her mother had phoned to invite her, two days ago, her mind had been so involved with erecting barriers against her heart's demands that she agree to marry Jackson that she hadn't had the mental reserves to call on to find a suitable excuse.

So she washed her hair in the new and very expensive shampoo she had treated herself to on the way home, took a leisurely bath, soaked every inch of herself with body lotion and went to bed to sleep the sleep of the profoundly happy and dream of the day when she would be Jackson's wife, going where he went, encouraging his very considerable talent, selling his drawings on street corners when they were broke—and when he wasn't looking, of course—to pay for their next meal or night's lodgings!

She woke early, refreshed and bright-eyed. Excitement curled through her, leaving a wake of heady delight. Later today she would go to Jackson, but first she would be able to tell Miranda the news. She would do it over lunch, and Lily would know too, and that would ensure that everyone else in the area would know by the end of the day.

And she would be able to tell Jackson that the whole town knew about them, that she'd already

handed in her resignation, and that would make
him realise that she knew her own mind, that she
didn't care if the whole town gasped and threw up
its collective hands in horror at the thought of the
so-sensible S. Bryce-Jones tossing her secure future
to the winds and hitching her life to a charming
wanderer who had nothing but a pair of talented
hands and a distant dream.

She wore her usual sensible summer-weight
business gear, but left her heavy, slippery hair
loose because Jackson liked it that way and she'd
be thinking of him. After work she would change
into something feminine and floaty—one of the
dresses she'd bought at the local boutique and
hadn't worn yet.

Contrary to her expectations, the morning flew
by, news of her forthcoming resignation causing a
ripple on the placid surface of the sober banking
establishment. But the ripples didn't touch her,
nothing could touch her now, and she walked into
the lounge bar of the Feathers feeling ten feet tall.
And beautiful.

Miranda and Lily were already waiting, sitting at
a table by one of the bow-fronted windows, glasses
of gin and tonic in front of them on the highly
polished round table. Lily had had a blue rinse
since Susanna had seen her last, and it didn't suit
her, but Miranda, as always, looked like an
advertisement for the beauty industry.

'Darling——' Miranda handed her the lunch
menu. 'Lily and I have already ordered. You're
late; we'd begun to give up hope.'

She was late because she'd stopped to buy
perfume and a new lipstick, but she wasn't going
to explain that. Taking a sip of the tomato juice
she'd brought over from the bar—she didn't need

alcohol, she was high on happiness—she smiled beautifully. 'I hope you'll find my news worth waiting for. I'm going to marry Jackson Arne.' And that should wipe the patronising smile from her mother's face!

'But darling—how absolutely fantastic!'

If Miranda were acting for Lily's benefit, then she was doing it extremely well, and Susanna had to shake herself to make sure she wasn't dreaming when her mother burbled on, looking over-the-moon, 'When? Have you set the date yet? My goodness, there'll be so much to arrange! And you must promise, dear, to bring him over for dinner soon. Very soon. Well, isn't this fabulous news, Lily? Mind you, I'm not in the least surprised—I guessed which way the wind was blowing!'

Lily was looking shattered, but pleased, too, and Susanna couldn't understand it. But Lily couldn't know that Miranda had threatened to cut her daughter out of her will, disown her, if Jackson Arne so much as mentioned marriage. So Lily was probably only looking pleased because Miranda was making it sound like her ugly duckling daughter had just landed the catch of the century. She must be thinking that the unknown, to her, Jackson Arne was even more socially acceptable than the spurned Edmond!

In a complete daze, Susanna gave her order—smoked trout pâté with salad—and didn't even feel one quiver of apprehension at the thought that Miranda would turn all venomous and disgusted as soon as she got her on her own. The delighted act was for Lily's benefit. Miranda wouldn't want the whole town to know how strongly she disapproved of everthing about Jackson Arne. She was buying time, waiting for the opportunity to get her,

Susanna, on her own. And then all hell would be
let loose! But nothing her mother said or threatened
would have any effect. She was going to marry
Jackson, and nothing would make her change her
mind.

Even so, she was grateful for the reprieve when
she had to leave to get back to the bank. Lily
showed no sign of rushing off and leaving her
alone with her mother, and Susanna left them
lashing out on brandies to go with their coffee.

She practically ran all the way home after leaving
the bank early because she couldn't bear to delay
seeing Jackson for one moment longer than was
necessary. But she made time to have a quick bath
to rid herself of the day's stickiness, was lavish
with the new perfume and pleased with the
reflection that smiled back at her from the full-
length mirror in her bedroom.

Her dress was fine cotton voile, sleeveless, cut in
a low scoop at the front and back, the bodice
slightly bloused above a floaty skirt. The pattern of
smudgy lemon yellow flowers on a delicate cream
background suited her colouring, made her skin
look glowing. She didn't wear a bra because hers
were all rather voluminously cut with serviceable,
wide shoulder straps which would have shown
around the edges of the scoopy top of the dress.
Soon she would buy pretty, sexy underwear,
nightwear too, and she knew that Jackson would
agree that the money was better spent that way
than hoarded for a rainy day.

There was a latent sensuality about her, an
earthiness, that hadn't been there before as she
brushed her hair until it looked like spun silk and
applied the new lipstick and a hint of green
eyeshadow. Then, feeling as though she might

burst with the pressure of her inner happiness, she set out across the sunny meadow.

The cottage looked like a sleepy animal, basking under the cloudless blue sky. There was no sound but the peaceful call of a wood pigeon and the muffled drum beat of her own anticipating heart. And then there was the sharp ringing of metal against stone, and she knew that he was there.

Skirting the cottage, making for the makeshift studio, Susanna felt suddenly, absurdly nervous. And the sight of him, stripped to the waist, his tanned skin glistening with sweat, made her mouth go dry. He was so perfect to look at; there was strength, grace, fluidity, in every movement as he wielded the steel hammer and steel points against the marble. How could he possibly want her— plain, sensible, big-Susanna, to share his life?

But she wasn't plain—Jackson had told her so in no uncertain terms—and she certainly wasn't behaving sensibly now, not in the accepted sense of the word, she wasn't. She was beautiful in his eyes, and she loved him, and the rest of the world could go hang because, at last, she knew what she wanted and was going to take it, greedily, eagerly.

Her feet made no sound as she approached him, or any sound she did make was drowned by the ring of steel on stone. But even though he didn't turn around, she knew he knew she was there because, just for a second, his swinging rhythm faltered before he applied himself to his task with increased concentration.

Standing close to him, her heart picked up speed, racing, the palms of her hands growing wet with perspiration. She ached to reach out and touch him but was paralysed by the strange shyness that still possessed her. And why, dear God why, didn't he stop work, look at her, say just one word of greeting? He must know why she had come!

But did he? He had asked her to think carefully about his proposal, to find him and tell him when she'd decided. He'd said he would put no more pressure on—it was up to her. For all he knew, she might have come to tell him that she'd thought about it and wouldn't marry him if he were the last man alive.

Her heart swelled with love as she thought about his possible apprehension, and she cast around for something to say to ease them gently together, over the awkward moment which shouldn't have been awkward but was.

Watching him work, she was proud of what he was doing, a little awed by it. He was creating a masterpiece, wresting an image of beauty out of the stone with sweat and love and deep sensitivity. And even if he weren't famous now, he would be one day, he couldn't fail, and, huskily, she told him so and he threw back his head and laughed. And the sound was unpleasant, grating.

Jackson put his tools down and she watched with troubled eyes as he wiped the sweat from his face with a rag he pulled out of the pocket in his jeans. He was like a stranger. She felt she didn't know him at all. It frightened her.

'So you consider I'm a good risk now, do you?'

His words were unpleasant, too. They held a bitterness she couldn't understand. How could he possibly object to her sincere comment about his one-day fame and fortune?

Susanna shivered suddenly, her eyes clouding with anxiety as she saw that his face was bone-white beneath his tan, the green eyes that had never seemed cold before now like glaciers. She didn't know what was wrong, but she had to tell him of how her love for him had grown until it had burst the bounds of her only previous allies—her reason and common sense. Perhaps then this hard-eyed stranger would look more like the Jackson she loved.

But her words faltered, dying away in her throat as someone—a girl's voice—called, 'Jacks, darling man, if you don't come in and eat this mess, I'm going to throw it in the bin!'

And the blonde she'd seen him with before, on that rainy day in the High Street, came round the corner. She had tied her long riotous hair on top of her head in an attractively precarious mass, she was holding a pan in which a soggy omelette reposed, and her tanned and slender but curvy body was clad in a tiny bra and a pair of wispy briefs—very partially covered by the smallest, frilliest, silliest apron Susanna had ever seen.

Susanna's face was ashen, and she felt cold. She was shaking inside, and she knew that if she didn't remove herself at once she would find herself doing something she'd regret for the rest of her life. Like killing someone.

It was an effort to make her lips move, but she managed, 'I'm sorry, I obviously called at an inopportune moment,' before blundering off across the meadow, her temples throbbing with pain and jealousy. Searing, sickening, violent jealousy.

Jackson's strange behaviour, his hardness, was explained now, at least she thought it was. Sheer embarrassment at having her pick that very moment to choose to see him explained his aggressive attitude. She had walked in on him when he'd been entertaining a little playmate—and it hurt,

dear God it hurt! She had never imagined she
could feel so much pain.

He was a very physical man. He would always
need a woman in his life. But why—*why* couldn't
he have waited?

'Not so fast!'

He had caught up with her before she'd tottered
a dozen yards, grabbing her arm, pulling her round
to face him. She hadn't expected him to follow;
she had imagined he'd be too ashamed of himself.
And the fact that he had gave her just a little hope
that he might have an explanation.

Tears of pain and humiliation were already
sparkling in her eyes, and they began to fall in
earnest when she saw how he dropped her arms,
wiping the palms of his hands down the sides of his
jeans as if to erase the touch of her.

'I came to tell you I'd marry you,' she told him
through quivering lips, feeling betrayed and ill.
'I've even given in my resignation to the bank,
and——'

'I just bet you have,' he drawled acidly, his eyes
transfixing her, and she blurted.

'And all the time you'd got—got that near-naked
girl with you! And I've seen you with her before,
so don't try to pass her off as the home help!'

She wanted to stamp her feet and wail, but that
would be childish. She also desperately wanted him
to reassure her, tell her that the curvy little blonde
was someone he'd hired to do the cooking and
housework, someone who took all her clothes off
on the merest whim because she was touched in
the head, but harmless. And that was just as
childish because it wouldn't, *couldn't*, be anything
like that.

And Jackson wasn't in a reassuring mood,

because he didn't mention the blonde, or try to excuse her undressed presence. All he said was—cutting the last stanchion of hope from beneath her feet, 'Forget I ever mentioned marriage. I don't want to set eyes on you again. Oh, and by the way,' he was already turning, on his way back to the cottage, adding the afterthought, 'when you see your mother, tell her not to bother to come out here to apologise to me. I might just forget what a gentleman I am if she did.'

Susanna, white-faced with the shock of all that had happened since she'd set out with such happiness in her heart, could only echo hollowly, 'Apologise?' She flicked her tongue over her parched lips. Suddenly, she had to know. She was having suspicions she couldn't begin to cope with. He was going, but her voice, harsh with her urgency, stopped him. 'What would she have to apologise for?'

'Nothing much.' His powerful naked shoulders lifted in a wry shrug, and the face he turned to her was empty of expression. 'She dropped by one afternoon early this week, looking as if she might catch something nasty from being around me. She instructed me to stay away from you. She told me that she and your father would cut you off without a penny of the considerable family fortune if you were ever foolish enough to marry me.'

He walked away then, swinging effortlessly through the meadow grass, his golden head held high as if he hadn't a care in the world. And she heard him call out, most amiably—as if he'd just had an unpleasant duty to perform and was relieved it was over—'Fran, my love, I'll eat that mess you've cooked up now, if you'll promise something delectable for afters!' and he really sounded as if he were looking forward to what the undressed blonde could offer in the way of afters!

He didn't look back, and Susanna was glad of that. She couldn't have done a thing to hide her distress from him. Her legs wouldn't hold her; they gave way beneath the weight of her misery and she sank to the ground in a heap, clutching her arms around her knees, her face buried in the skirts of her pretty dress as she rocked herself back and forth, giving way completely to the pain of knowing that he had only been interested in her prospects, after all.

One hint from Miranda that Jackson could never hope to gain financially by marrying her daughter had been enough to have him looking as if he hated the sight of her.

Miranda had said that when he knew he would gain nothing by marrying her daughter, they would all be able to sit back and see how fast he could run. Well, he was running now.

CHAPTER TEN

SUSANNA walked into her house like an automaton. She had no recollection of how long she'd crouched in the meadow, weeping as though her heart would break.

Perhaps her heart was dead, like a stone. She felt nothing, just empty. Miranda had been right all along. Jackson had wooed her, pursued her, teased, flattered, made love to her. And all because he'd done some snooping around and discovered that, some day, she'd be one hell of a wealthy lady. And one succinct word from Miranda had killed all his reasons for wanting to marry her stone dead. If she were to be disinherited, disowned, Jackson didn't want to know her.

Even now she could hardly believe it of him, and she didn't know whether she hated her mother or not. Because if Jackson hadn't found out until after they'd been married she would at least have had a little happiness to remember.

It was growing dusk, and she flicked lights on as she walked through the little house on leaden legs. And when the phone shrilled out she picked it up, because she was doing things automatically, not thinking. And she almost slammed it down again when she heard Miranda's voice, only she didn't have the wits or the energy to do anything as positive as that.

'Darling—I've been trying to reach you for hours,' her mother burbled ecstatically. 'I would have hung around until you'd left the bank, but Daddy has one of his Medal Society thingies this evening and I'd promised to do the eats. We can't trust Mrs Hobbs to do anything like that these days; she's only good for the rough, poor old thing. Anyway, I simply had to talk to you about your stupendous news. Daddy's thrilled, needless to say!'

Susanna blinked. Her stomach muscles clenching in reaction to the sudden pain inside her. She was beginning to come alive again and she didn't want to. The numbness had been so much easier to cope with.

Bewildered, she held the receiver out in front of her, staring at it. Had her mother gone mad? Or had she? Frowning, she held the instrument to her ear again, and she wasn't hearing things. Miranda was almost hysterical in her delight, and it didn't add up to what she knew of her parents' feelings about Jackson Arne, or to what Jackson had said about Miranda's visit to him earlier that week.

'I've got to hand it to you, you clever thing! And fancy not telling me! Letting me make such a fool of myself! Still, I'll forgive you! Now, darling, about the arrangements for the wedding——' Miranda gave a breathy gurgle of laughter. 'Darling, I can't think straight! I'm still reeling from what happened this morning,' Miranda gushed on, regardless of the stony silence at the other end of the line. 'When Lily and I walked into the Feathers this morning your Jackson was there, and I thought, I wonder what *he's* doing here, and then Lily went over and spoke to him—you know the gushy way she does—anyway, while Lily and I were having our drinks she told me all. She and Henry have known the Arnes for years—only very vaguely, mind you; they're not on calling terms. Fancy Jackson's father being a baronet! The thirteenth baronet Arne, no less! So you'll be Lady Arne one day, Jackson being the only son and all that. Apparently, his father, Sir Bertram Arne, is elderly, practically in his dotage, and his mother died absolutely ages ago so you'll be able to take your position of lady of Arne Hall straight away. And according to Lily, Arne Hall is reputed to be out of this world—packed with positive *treasures*. Mind you, Lily tells me your Jackson isn't exactly on the breadline—though you'll know all about that, you sly boots! Who would think, to look at him, that he's world-famous, that his work fetches enormous sums of money? The dear boy looks as if he hasn't a penny to bless himself with—but then the upper classes can get away with that sort of thing, can't they, dear? And of course,' her voice lowered to a conspiratorial whisper, all-girls-together-and-any-thing-goes, 'I don't know whether you already know this, but according to Lily, who makes it her business to know all there is to know about anyone who's remotely interesting in a hundred mile radius, your Jackson's been dead set against marriage—much to Sir Bertram's distress—for simply years. And I suppose, when one looks at it from his point of view, one can understand it. He's so eligible—good-looking, talented, extremely wealthy and in line for a title. Impeccable breeding, my dear. Impeccable. Apparently, he was almost at the altar once—about ten years ago—then he found out that the girl in question was more interested in the family title and money than she was in him. It quite put him off marriage—so you've been doubly clever to land him, haven't you, dear?'

Miranda paused briefly for breath, then rushed on. 'Now, have you dear young things fixed a date for the wedding yet? September would be nice, don't you think? Early September? And would you bring Jackson over for dinner on Saturday evening? Sir Bertram, too, if you could possibly persuade him. Daddy and I would be most happy if he would stay overnight, and we could run him back to Arne Hall on Sunday, make a day of it.'

Susanna swallowed, the throat action painful. Her knuckles showed white as she gripped the receiver, her mind staggering under the weight of what she had heard. No wonder her mother had changed her tune and was now singing like a demented canary. But she had to be sure she was getting the facts straight. Keeping her voice level, she asked, 'Did you speak to Jackson this morning, at the Feathers?'

'Speak to him?' Miranda sounded a mite affronted. 'Naturally. I didn't know, then, that he'd actually asked you to marry him, but I did know you'd been seeing quite a lot of the dear boy—what with posing for him, and everything. But——' Her voice hesitated for a second, then she burbled on, not admitting to having put a foot wrong, because the way she always saw it, she never did. 'After Lily had told me who he actually *was*, I did go over to him and ask him to join us. I told him that we were expecting you shortly. But he said he had an appointment, and left. Pity. We could all have had a nice little engagement celebration. And talking about that, when are you choosing the ring? Or is it to be a family heirloom? And you haven't said yet when the wedding's to be. Really, Susanna, for a girl who's just caught the man of the decade, you're being remarkably mum and morose!'

Her mother's reply to her question had told her all she wanted to know. It was the final piece of the jigsaw, and it fell into place with a sound like the crack of doom. She said heavily, 'I've got a message for you from Jackson. He says you're not to trouble yourself to apologise to him. He might forget he's a gentleman if you do,' and put the phone down.

As she had known it would, the phone screamed out again almost immediately and Miranda's voice came darkly, as if there had been no interruption. 'What did he mean by that?'

'Do you really need an answer?' Susanna felt immensely tired. She was going to bed, and she wouldn't be sorry if she never woke up. 'And before you start ordering your mother-of-the-bride outfit, I ought to tell you the wedding's off. And I never want to hear another word about it from you.'

Susanna said goodbye to Mr and Mrs Ryan and closed the front door. The latch snicked hollowly. The house felt hollow too, echoing its occupant, and she would be glad when, a week today, she moved out. At least it looked as though she had found a purchaser for Mallow Cottage. This was the third time the Ryans had been to look over it, and they seemed keen. He was a retired fishmonger from Birmingham and they both wanted to move to the country; Mallow Cottage would be exactly right for them.

And she would be moving to London, sharing a flat with a girl friend from the old days while she looked around for a place of her own, looked for work. A job shouldn't be too difficult; she had an interview with a firm of merchant bankers a week on Tuesday. The position would offer a greater challenge and a higher income, and she was fairly confident of the outcome. Confident, but not terribly interested. Nothing seemed to interest her these days, not since Jackson had left.

He had gone on the day after he'd told her he never wanted to set eyes on her again, on a warm late-July evening, in the lavender twilight. She had heard a lorry rumbling by, negotiating the green lane with care, the unfinished Venus strapped on, covered with a tarpaulin. He had been following on a powerful-looking motor bike, and the curvy blonde, Fran, had been riding pillion, laughing, clinging on to him.

That had been two months ago. He had gone, taking her heart with him, and although she'd tried to forget him, write the whole episode off as experience, she couldn't do it.

The September evening was chilly with the foretaste of autumn sharpening the air, and Susanna draped a nut-brown cashmere shawl over the floaty cream and black Indian cotton dress she was wearing and went outside, too restless to stay indoors.

Since Jackson had left she had taken trouble with her appearance, spending more on clothes than she had ever done before, experimenting with make-up. It would be all too easy to let herself slip into a limbo of not caring about anything. She owed it to herself and, in a quirky kind of way, felt she owed it to Jackson, too. He had opened her eyes to her own potential, making her see that she could be beautiful.

Jackson. Jackson Arne. The echo of his name, her memory of him, filled her head to the exclusion of almost everything else. She recalled how, on the evening they'd first met, she'd had the feeling that she'd heard his name before, that it was familiar. And now, when it was all too late, she recalled— years ago—having flipped through an article on the promising young sculptor in one of her father's Sunday supplements. She'd been at home for the Christmas holidays, in her first year at the LSE, and she hadn't been overly interested in the arts; she'd been too preoccupied with her own career prospects in the world of finance.

Not that it would have made any difference if she had remembered at the time when they'd first met. She would have told him that she'd heard of him, knew who he was. And he would have immediately been on his guard because he had had one nasty experience with a woman who'd only wanted him for who he was and not what he was.

He might still have pursued her, because he had wanted her, she knew that, but he wouldn't have asked her to marry him. And once his desire for her had been slaked, he would have tossed her aside.

Her feet had carried her beyond her garden, across the green lane and through the gate to the field she would always think of as Jackson's meadow. She was going to the cottage where he had stayed for a few short weeks. The experience would be unproductive—backward glances always were—but for this one last time she would allow her heart to overrule her common sense.

It was just as she remembered it, but the soul of the little house was gone. The cluttered, ugly furniture was still in place, even the untidy piles of books still littered the floor. But Jackson wasn't here, and never would be again, and so the life had left it.

Shivering with her melancholy thoughts, Susanna knelt on the rug in front of the empty hearth and pushed the kindling from a bucket she'd found in an alcove into the grate, on top of some sheets of newspaper she'd crumpled into loose balls. She found matches on the mantelpiece and the sticks were soon crackling, casting moving, flickering shadows on the whitewashed walls, the crowding furniture.

It had been easier, in a way, when, briefly, in between the moment when he'd told her he didn't want to see her again and finding out, from Miranda, exactly who he was, she had been able to hate him for the callous fortune-hunter she'd believed him to be. Hatred was easier to bear than this despairing misery.

She had tried to hate him for believing she had only agreed to marry him after she'd learned who he was. But she was fair-minded, and couldn't. She, loving him, had believed the worst of him, so she couldn't blame him for doing precisely the same in regard to herself, could she? If only he had been here that evening when she had come over to tell him she'd marry him! None of this would have happened. How drastically twenty-four hours could change one's life!

Everything was terrible beyond belief. Life was a mess. But it had to go on, so they said, though Susanna couldn't think why.

Curled up on the hearth rug, staring into the flames, she knew she was sufficiently strong-minded to go on without him. But just for this one last time she was remembering, losing herself in bitter sweet thoughts of what might have been. So that when she heard the creak of the opening door, heard Jackson's voice speak her name, it seemed natural to her, just for a second, because the presence of him she had been conjuring out of her memories was totally real, expected.

She turned her head slowly, her limbs tense, her eyes widening as the shock of her situation hit her. She was hurting inside and the hurting would go on, increase; he would see to that. Because whatever reason he had for coming here, it hadn't been to find her.

He had almost certainly come for something he'd left behind when he'd vacated the premises so hurriedly, and seeing her here, where she had no right to be, would disgust him—believing what he did of her.

Jackson hadn't moved since he'd spoken her name. He stood just inside the door, looking as if he'd seen a ghost. And perhaps he had. The ghost of a lost love. Although he had never said he loved her. Perhaps he didn't know how to love. But he had wanted her body—enough, in the end, to offer to marry her. And he would have known, then, that she hadn't been about to marry him for his possessions, his standing.

Only that had been before Lily and Miranda had done the damage, and now it was too late because he would be thinking she was like the other girl. And who knew what went on behind those shadowed eyes, eyes that were fixed on her with an intensity she found frightening? There were lines of strain on his face that hadn't been there before; he looked older, harder, tougher.

Any minute now he was going to ask her what the hell she was doing here, and she had to get out, fast, because she couldn't handle any more pain.

Susanna scrambled to her feet, wrapping her shawl tightly around her, her heart hammering. He believed the worst of her, and he looked as though he hated her; she wondered how many other girls had shared the big man's bed since she'd seen him last. Or perhaps the little blonde, Fran, was staying the course. And she had to say something, anything, because this aching silence was absurd and dreadful, like something in a terrible doom-ridden Russian play.

'I'm sorry,' she heard the hesitancy in her voice, dealt with it, and continued much more firmly, 'I shouldn't be here. Just passing——' and seeing the fire, would he swallow that? 'I'll leave you in peace.' She was moving to the door, on her way, but it didn't look as if he would stand aside and let her pass. The smile she dredged up from somewhere was small and tight. 'I expect you want to look for whatever it was you left behind.'

'You'll never leave me in peace, and I've found what I left behind.'

His voice was harsh, tinged with bitterness, and his height and breadth, the black sweater and jeans he wore, made him menacing as he closed in, reducing the space between them to a hair's breadth.

Susanna moved back instinctively, her breath coming jerkily, but his hands caught her, his fingers biting into the flesh of her shoulders, sliding down her arms to capture her wrists when she raised her hands to beat him off.

'Changed your mind, sweet?' he bit out savagely. 'I haven't. I still want you. I've tried to forget you, but you give me no peace.'

He was going to make love to her, she could read his intention in his eyes, and she knew that if he did, in this mood of hatred, she would die of misery and shame. If he wanted to punish her, he couldn't come up with a better way if he thought about it for a thousand years.

He was close enough for her to feel the heat of his desire and she shuddered, the fight suddenly draining out of her. She closed her eyes so that he wouldn't see her defeat. But he saw the tears that trickled beneath her lids, because his voice changed, roughened slightly, as he pulled her to him, cradling her, his arms like bands of steel.

'Not tears. I can't think straight if you cry.'

She heard the anguish in his voice and she melted against him, loving him, a sob rising to choke her as she heard the bleakness in his voice. 'You're like a madness in my mind, and it won't let go. It grows and grows until I can do nothing.'

There was pain to be assuaged, and she could do that for him, but was she strong enough, unselfish enough, to bear her own pain when it was over? She met his shadowed eyes unwillingly. 'What do you suggest we do about it?'

'We marry.'

Those two words, their harsh, unloving delivery, burned into her brain, and she searched his stony face and found nothing.

He had himself firmly under control, the pain, if it was still there, expertly hidden. He took her hand, idly almost. 'We have to talk.'

'I don't think so.' She tried to snatch her hand back but his grip tightened painfully. There was nothing to say that hadn't already been said. 'You said it all the day I came here and found you with that woman. Fran. You called her Fran,' she threw at him as he tugged her towards the fireside.

'Fran is my sister.' Jackson's eyes flickered over her narrowly as he pulled her down on the hearth rug beside him. 'She seems to think I can't look after myself, so she moved in to make sure that I got enough to eat, as you'd refused to do it,' he taunted.

Tight-lipped, Susanna watched as he flung a log on the fire, setting sparks flying up the chimney. Her eyes were hard. He had put her through a living hell of jealousy.

'You didn't tell me! You let me believe——'

'That she was my live-in woman,' he took her up edgily. 'Sure I did. Why not? I wanted to make you hurt as I was hurting. My God, how do you think I felt when you came trotting over here, all bright-eyed and bushy-tailed, to tell me you'd graciously accept my proposal of marriage? When I knew darned well you'd resisted me all along the line, clung to your engagement to the safe, dull Edmond, and had only decided I was a good enough risk—better even than Edmond—after you'd learned who I was from your mother and the Anstruther woman!'

'But——'

Susanna wanted to tell him the truth, although she doubted he'd ever believe it, but he laid a finger against her lips, silencing her, her mouth quivering under his touch.

'I'm trying not to mind, trying to accept it. Don't make it more difficult for me by telling me things you think I want to hear, things I couldn't begin to believe, under the circumstances that arose that day.'

His finger slid down, hooking beneath her chin,

tilting her face to his waiting lips. He brushed hers lightly, the movement silky, tormenting, his hands moving down over her shoulders, cupping her breasts, and a low whimper was torn from her as his mouth hardened, probing intimately, until she thought she would die from the pleasure he was giving her. He broke the kiss, his breathing ragged.

'I can't do without you. I've tried, but you walked into my life and took over. And what it comes down to in the end is a matter of trust.'

The log in the hearth flared, the firelight flickering over his face, accentuating the hard planes, throwing his eyes into shadow, masking them. He caught her hands between his, pulling them up to lie on his chest, and she could feel the heavy pounding of his heart beneath the covering of fine black wool.

'I made demands—asked you to take me on trust, deliberately let you think I had nothing to offer but the man I am. But I didn't trust you enough to believe that you would have agreed to marry me whatever my circumstances. I've been working on it, sweet,' his voice thickened as he reached out for her, dragging her to him, burying his head against her breasts. 'Believing you would only come to me if you had proof that I was a good enough risk was bad enough. The thought of doing without you for the rest of my life is even worse. I can't. I love you, Susanna, and I'll take you on any terms.'

An astounded smile lightened her face, banishing the strain of the last few weeks as she tangled her fingers in his bright hair. Everything was going to be all right! The agony had been worth it in the end. All she had to do was convince him of the truth, because although he'd said he'd take her on any terms, and that only made her love him more, he deserved to know what had really happened.

She felt light-headed as her fingers moved softly, adoringly, over his face, and her voice was husky as she told him, 'You were testing me, and I didn't fail. Believe me, I didn't fail. You talk of trust— you have to trust me on this.'

'I told you, I'm trying. But what else was I to think when you clung to Edmond for dear life? The last time I went to your house, the day I asked you to marry me, you were letting him make love to you. Even when I'd proved to you over and over again that you wanted me! And you came to me only after you'd met your mother for lunch that day and she'd told you who I was. I know she must have done because when she asked me to join her and the Anstruther woman, adding that they were expecting you at any moment, she couldn't have been nicer,' he muttered thickly, his words muffled against the softness of her breasts. 'Every time I'd met your mother before, including the time when she came here to try to warn me off, she'd looked at me as if I was poison. But after the Anstruther woman had put her right she couldn't have been more charming. And I went home feeling sick all over. I didn't want to think you'd come haring straight over, and when you did I knew——'

'You know nothing,' Susanna butted in firmly. This had gone far enough. She had gone over it numberless times in her mind during the past dreadful weeks, and she knew, only too well, how the evidence added up against her. 'By the time I knew exactly who you were, what your circumstances were, you'd already told me you never wanted to see me again. I even spent a few terrible hours thinking you'd only been after me for what you thought I would one day inherit,' she confessed. 'You said Miranda had been to see you, to say she'd cut me off without a penny, and I immediately thought the worst.'

'She did worry me,' Jackson said soberly, his eyes holding hers. 'Not for the reasons she had in mind—I'm well able to support you—but I knew the pressure would be well and truly on you then, it would be one more reason for you to refuse to give up your security for love. She gave me a few sleepless nights wondering if what I knew you felt for me was strong enough. And explain what you mean by saying you didn't know who I was until after you'd come here,' he added tersely.

Susanna's mouth curved in a slow, sweet smile,

'I knew nothing until much later that evening when Miranda phoned. I'd been sitting out in that field, howling my head off because I thought you'd only wanted to marry me for my prospects and as soon as you'd found out I wouldn't have any because I'd be disinherited if I married you, you'd cancelled your offer and invited Fran to move in. Anyway——' She couldn't help smiling; all the trauma seemed so long ago and unimportant now. 'Mother was all agog to tell all, as you can well imagine, and what she had to say shook me rigid! Although I should have guessed something of the sort when she was so delighted when I told her and Lily over lunch that I was going to marry you. I didn't understand it until much later—I'd been expecting her to throw hysterics of quite another kind.'

His head came up.

'You really did tell her before you knew who I

was? Before you'd even told me?' Incredulity was in his voice, and something else. Joy?

'I did,' she told him softly, finding it difficult to speak at all because she seemed to be melting all over, disintegrating with her love for him. 'I—I also gave in my resignation at the bank, the day before, actually, and came to see you that evening, but there was a note pinned to the door—'

Jackson groaned, and she knew what he was thinking, that if he hadn't been out, then none of this would have happened. 'I'd gone over to fetch Fran—'

'It doesn't matter. Not now. I just want to tell you that I broke my engagement to Edmond before I came to pose for you. What you saw was Edmond trying to make me change my mind. I'd been fighting him off, hating every minute.'

He received her words in silence, and the silence stretched. Taut. There was a battle going on inside his head and when he took her face between his hands his eyes bored into hers, trying to reach her soul.

'Why didn't you tell me you'd finished with Edmond?' His voice was tight. 'Why let me beat my head against a wall?'

'Because, to be honest, I was afraid.' Susanna turned her head in his hands, just slightly, her mouth moving against his palm, and she heard his tugged-in breath, short and ragged, and murmured, 'I knew I couldn't marry him; I knew what you did to me. And it scared me. Even after I knew I was in love with you I was afraid. I had a lifetime of conditioning to climb over. I'd been made to believe, almost since birth, that all I had going for me was my brain and my common sense. Famous for it, I was. And then you made me see myself

differently, as a woman—even a beautiful woman—
but I still had my ingrained common sense to deal
with before I could admit to myself that the world
could be well lost for love. And you didn't help.
You put obstacles in my way at every turn. I had
to fight the battle on my own. No help from you—
letting me think you were a shiftless hobo. How
you must have laughed when I babbled on about
selling your drawings to make some cash, how
you'd be famous one day!'

'I didn't laugh, sweet. Your concern touched me
deeply and I almost came clean, but it had become
something of a matter of principle by then. I
needed to know you'd take me on any terms at all.
Because on the night you posed for me I knew I
loved you. I'd been attracted to you on sight.
When I saw you walking in the water in the
moonlight, I knew you were the most beautiful
thing I'd ever seen. I probably loved you from that
moment—I've certainly never pursued a woman
before. If a woman's offered, I've taken. No
strings, no commitments, certainly no pursuit on
my part—I saved my energy for my work. But
there I was, chasing after a woman who clearly
found me an embarrassment, who was engaged to
someone else . . . What else could it have been
but love? But I didn't have the sense to realise it
at the time. I told myself I was concerned about
you, about the way you put yourself down, hid the
real and very lovely Susanna behind that prim,
ultra-respectable lady bank manager image you
seemed so fond of. And I knew, when I finally
faced the fact of my love for you, that I'd have
one hell of a job getting you to admit you loved
me, too, that you'd marry me even though you
thought I hadn't got a bean——'

'And all that because you were afraid of being married for your material assets,' she chided gently. She snuggled into the curve of his arm, teasing, 'How very stupid you must be! Don't you know how gorgeous you are? Possessions don't come into it.'

'It took you long enough to reach that conclusion,' he reminded her drily.

'Ah—but I'm not your usual run-of-the-mill girl.' Susanna lifted appealing eyes to his, raising her hand to trace the curve of his lips with a quivering finger, her heart bursting with love for him. 'I'm far more sensible than most. I brought myself up that way.'

'You're a minx and a baggage.' Strong white teeth nipped her exploring finger. 'And far from run-of-the-mill. And I know just how sensible you liked to think you were, so I know what a battle you must have had. And that makes me a happy and humble man.'

His lips moved against her hair, trailing down to find the sensitive underside of her jaw as his hands began to move seductively over her body, sure fingers finding the tiny fabric-covered buttons at the front of her dress.

Susanna, her heart taking up the now familiar breathless tattoo, took herself most firmly in hand, positively for the last time, she promised herself. But there was something she had to know, and if Jackson undressed her, as was his clear intention, she would lose the power of speech, of thought. Placing her hands firmly over his, she stayed his busy fingers.

'Were you very much in love with the girl you were engaged to once? The one who soured you where marriage was concerned?'

Her head was bent in cowardly fashion, her hair swinging forward to hide her expression, because he must have loved her very much—he wouldn't have been so embittered if that weren't the case. And although it was in the past, having him admit it would hurt, and she'd have to cope with that alone, without his eyes on her. And it wouldn't take long to get over the pain of knowing he'd loved so very deeply, because it was old history now.

'You talk too much. For a woman with such magnificent child-bearing hips you talk altogether too much! And why dig into the past, when the future looks so enticing?'

'I want to know. She was indirectly responsible for so much of the misery of the last few weeks,' Susanna said with great determination, her lower lip protruding stubbornly as her eyes slanted up, around the curtain of her hair, to lock with his.

Jackson sighed in fine melodramatic fashion, his voice pained. 'You're going to give me a difficult time; I can see that. Never tangle with a strong-minded woman—that's what my old granny used to say, and look at where it's got me—cowed, subservient . . .'

But there was nothing remotely cowed or subservient about the way his hands continued their roving possession of her body, inducing hers to do the same to his. And she had great difficulty concentrating on what he was saying; all her attention was on what he was doing—and she began to wish she'd kept her mouth shut, because he seemed prepared to spin it out all night, and his hands were making her see that words weren't what she wanted at all . . .

'Like most parents,' he began pontifically, 'my

father wanted to see me settled, with a suitable wife, who would give me children to carry on his line. My mother died when I was twelve, and my father is actually old enough to be my grandfather—they married late in life. So, when I got to what he considered to be marriageable age, Father, with the help of a conniving aunt or two, began surrounding me with suitable girls. I had only just finished my art training, and I wasn't in the least interested in tying myself down. As I saw it, I had a whole lot of living to do. But Father began to get mildly paranoiac, and when Celia was invited along for a lazy summer weekend I remember thinking to myself that she'd do. She was two or three years older than I was, sophisticated, good to look at in a hard, brittle way. She was quite unlike the other little things that had been hauled out of the decaying woodwork of many an ancient family manor house, and I imagined myself in love with her. I say 'imagined' with hindsight. When it all fell through, after I'd discovered that she'd only been interested in the title and family wealth, my pride was the only thing that suffered.'

'She must have been a bitch,' Susanna interjected thickly, longing for the time when he would find other uses for his lips than word-forming. But she had asked to hear it, and she was sympathetic, and she couldn't understand any girl failing to be head over heels in love with him, just for himself.

'Not really. She was cool, calculating and she knew her own worth—but she wasn't an out-and-out bitch. When she married, she wanted to marry well, and that's all there was to it. But I made a bit of a song and dance about it,' Jackson grinned wryly, reminiscently. 'It was one way of getting Father and several interested old aunts to leave me in peace to get on with my work. My work was all that truly mattered to me, and it was easy to find female companionship if I wanted it. But it was always a no-strings, no commitments type of relationship because, by then, I'd discovered I was considered fair game by a great many females who wanted to gain financial security by way of a plain gold ring.' His hands dawdled up to frame her face, his eyes drowning with love. 'I had no intention of marrying; my way of life suited me fine. I have a studio at Arne, and the Dower House, a villa in Nice—and another studio—and you're going to love them both, sweet. I only borrowed this place because I needed to get right away at the time. I'd accepted the commission from Hugo because he badly wanted me to do it and he's an old and good friend, but I wasn't happy with it. So I needed a place where I could be completely alone to think, without hordes of friends dropping in as they tend to do in Nice, and hordes of delightful but slightly dotty relatives hanging around as they do when I'm at Arne. So I came here, and met you, and you changed my life, turned it inside out. But you were going to marry Edmond, who was suitable, and I could see that Miranda—I've already forgiven her, sweet, you've no need to worry about family feuds—whose influence over you was far too strong, thought I was the pits and far too lowly to be having anything at all to do with her nicely brought-up gel. So getting you to admit you loved me, despite my unsuitableness as it were, became an obsession. I wanted you so much, loved you so much, and I needed to know you were willing to come to me believing I had nothing to offer but my love.'

With a little help from her unthinking hands, he

had already removed her dress while he'd been talking, and he traced the edges of the wispy scraps of silk and lace that comprised her underwear. She saw his eyes flicker over the pale gleam of her body, touched by the fireglow.

'I've done all the talking I intend to do for quite some time to come,' he told her gruffly. 'Where we are about to go, sweet, words won't be necessary.'

Slowly, his head came down, his lips fusing with hers, and she lifted her arms, gathering him to her, pulling him closer. It was time to give, time to receive . . . with gladness and with love . . . the beginning of a whole new future, a whole new world. And she murmured throatily, 'Who needs words? Show me, my love.'

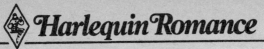
Harlequin Romance

Coming Next Month

2869 CARPENTARIA MOON Kerry Allyne
Photographer Eden arrives to be tourist director at an Australian cattle station, asked by Alick, a friend, but finds the station is owned by his older brother who regards her as the latest girlfriend Alick is trying to dump!

2870 WINNER TAKE ALL Kate Denton
When a campaign manager recommends that her boss, a Louisiana congressman, find a wife to dispel his playboy reputation, she never thinks she'll be the one tying the knot!

2871 FORCE FIELD Jane Donnelly
For a young amateur actress, playing Rosalind in an open-air production in Cornwall is enjoyable. But being emotionally torn between the estate owner's two sons, a sculptor and an artist, is distressing—until real love, as usual, settles the matter.

2872 THE EAGLE AND THE SUN Dana James
Jewelry designer Cass Elliott expects to enjoy a working holiday until her boss's son unexpectedly accompanies her and their arrival in Mexico proves untimely. She's excited by the instant rapport between herself and their Mexican host, then she learns that Miguel is already engaged....

2873 SHADOW FALL Rowan Kirby
Brought together by a young girl needing strong emotional support, a London schoolteacher and the pupil's widowed father fall in love. Then she learns of her resemblance to his deceased wife and can't help wondering if she's just a substitute.

2874 OFF WITH THE OLD LOVE Betty Neels
All of Rachel's troubles about being engaged to a TV producer who doesn't understand her nursing job and expects her to drop everything for his fashionable social life are confided to the comfortable Dutch surgeon, Radmer. Then, surprisingly, she finds Radmer is the man she loves!

Available in November wherever paperback books are sold, or through Harlequin Reader Service.

In the U.S.
901 Fuhrmann Blvd.
P.O. Box 1397
Buffalo, N.Y. 14240-1397

In Canada
P.O. Box 603
Fort Erie, Ontario
L2A 5X3

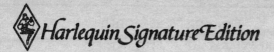

Harlequin Signature Edition

Penny Jordan

Stronger Than Yearning

He was the man of her dreams!

The same dark hair, the same mocking eyes; it was as if the
Regency rake of the portrait, the seducer of Jenna's dream, had
come to life. Jenna, believing the last of the Deverils dead, was
determined to buy the great old Yorkshire Hall—to claim it for
her daughter, Lucy, and put to rest some of the painful memories of Lucy's birth. She had no way of knowing that a direct des-
cendant of the black sheep Deveril even existed—or that James
Allingham and his own powerful yearnings would disrupt her
plan entirely.

Penny Jordan's first Harlequin Signature Edition *Love's Choices* was an
outstanding success. Penny Jordan has written more than 40 best-sell-
ing titles—more than 4 million copies sold.

Now, be sure to buy her latest bestseller, *Stronger Than Yearning*. Available wherever paperbacks are sold—in October.

ATTRACTIVE, SPACE SAVING BOOK RACK

Display your most prized novels on this handsome and sturdy book rack. The hand-rubbed walnut finish will blend into your library decor with quiet elegance, providing a practical organizer for your favorite hard-or soft-covered books.

Only $9.95

Approximately 16" x 8" when assembled

Assembles in seconds!

To order, rush your name, address and zip code, along with a check or money order for $10.70* ($9.95 plus 75¢ postage and handling) payable to *Harlequin Reader Service*:

Harlequin Reader Service
Book Rack Offer
901 Fuhrmann Blvd.
P.O. Box 1396
Buffalo, NY 14269-1396

Offer not available in Canada.

BKR-1A

*New York and Iowa residents add appropriate sales tax.

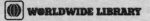